S0-AFX-558

CRITICAL ACCLAIM FOR
MARION CHESNEY'S NEW
POOR RELATION SERIES

LADY FORTESCUE STEPS OUT

"Chesney gives her many admirers a real treat with this first entry in [her new] series. She expertly sets the scene, recapturing the bawdiness and color of a long-ago time, and her characters fairly leap off the page. The 'poor relations' undergo adventures both hilarious and tragic; larceny, attempted murder, a love affair and unlikely alliances make the hotel the liveliest spot in London."

—*Publishers Weekly*

"This is a charming and humorous Regency, recommended for those who enjoy light-hearted historical romance."

—*Library Journal*

MISS TONKS TAKES A RISK

"This second volume of Chesney's latest series combines zany characters with light-hearted romance and a well-developed scenario to produce an engaging Regency. Followers of Chesney and Regency readers will enjoy."

—*Library Journal*

"I would never marry a lady who did not want me."

"How would you know?" asked Cassandra.

"Ladies swoon with delight when I approach them."

The hazel eyes studied Lord Eston's handsome face for a moment. "Yes, I suppose they would. You have a title and you are rich and you are not precisely an antidote."

"Alas, what can I say to move your heart?"

"Oh, tell the truth and admit you could not give a rap were my heart moved or not."

"I happen to find freckles very seductive."

"You are making fun of me."

"You are so blunt. Cannot you flirt?"

"I am very bad at it."

His eyes caressed her. "I would teach you. . . ."

**St. Martin's Paperbacks
by Marion Chesney**

PENELOPE
ANNABELLE
HENRIETTA

The House for the Season Series
THE MISER OF MAYFAIR (#1)
PLAIN JANE (#2)
THE WICKED GODMOTHER (#3)
RAKE'S PROGRESS (#4)
THE ADVENTURE (#5)
RAINBIRD'S REVENGE (#6)

The School for Manners Series
REFINING FELICITY (#1)
PERFECTING FIONA (#2)
ENLIGHTENING DELILAH (#3)
FINESSING CLARISSA (#4)
ANIMATING MARIA (#5)
MARRYING HARRIET (#6)

The Travelling Matchmaker
EMILY GOES TO EXETER (#1)
BELINDA GOES TO BATH (#2)
PENELOPE GOES TO PORTSMOUTH (#3)
BEATRICE GOES TO BRIGHTON (#4)
DEBORAH GOES TO DOVER (#5)
YVONNE GOES TO YORK (#6)

The Poor Relation Series
LADY FORTESCUE STEPS OUT
MISS TONKS TAKES A RISK
MRS. BUDLEY FALLS FROM GRACE
(coming in July 1994)

Miss Tonks Takes a Risk

(published in hardcover as Miss Tonks Turns to Crime)

BEING THE SECOND VOLUME OF THE POOR RELATION

Marion Chesney

ST. MARTIN'S PAPERBACKS

NOTE: If you purchased this book without a cover you should be aware that this book is stolen property. It was reported as "unsold and destroyed" to the publisher, and neither the author nor the publisher has received any payment for this "stripped book."

Miss Tonks Takes a Risk was previously published in hardcover under the title *Miss Tonks Turns to Crime*.

MISS TONKS TAKES A RISK

Copyright © 1993 by Marion Chesney.

Cover photograph by Wendi Schneider.

All rights reserved. No part of this book may be used or reproduced in any manner whatsoever without written permission except in the case of brief quotations embodied in critical articles or reviews. For information address St. Martin's Press, 175 Fifth Avenue, New York, NY 10010.

Library of Congress Catalog Card Number: 92-41837

ISBN 0-312-95219-8

Printed in the United States of America

St. Martin's Press hardcover edition/April 1993
St. Martin's Paperbacks edition/March 1994

10 9 8 7 6 5 4 3 2 1

FOR ANN ROBINSON AND HER DAUGHTER EMMA
WILSON, WITH LOVE.

Chapter One

Unless God send his hail,
Or blinding fire-balls, sleet or stifling snow,
In some time, his good time, I shall arrive.
—ROBERT BROWNING

MISS TONKS stepped into the waiting carriage as if stepping into a tumbril. Pale but brave, she sat down and lowered the glass and looked out at the faces of her friends standing outside the Poor Relation Hotel in London's Bond Street.

"I shall return with money," she said firmly.

"Do be careful," said little Mrs. Budley. "If it is too dangerous, simply come back to us. No one will reproach you."

"*I* shall," said the horrible Sir Philip Sommerville, looking more like an elderly tortoise than ever. "Just pick up some expensive geegaw, slip it in your reticule and make off."

Colonel Sandhurst looked at the sky as if for inspiration, as though he were mentally detaching himself from the whole distasteful project. Why could not Sir Philip himself go on a raiding mission? It was not fair of any of them. They had forced poor Miss Tonks into it.

"Courage," said Lady Fortescue, leaning on her ebony cane.

The carriage moved off. Miss Tonks's white handkerchief fluttered from the window in farewell.

Lady Fortescue, Sir Philip, Colonel Sandhurst and Mrs. Budley retreated into the Poor Relation and up to their private sitting-room.

The oddly assorted group had met some time ago. All of them had been poor relations, the genteel paupers of society, living on little more than their dignity. They had banded together and had started the Poor Relation Hotel, money for the venture having been supplied by Sir Philip Sommerville, who had stolen a vastly valuable necklace from the Duke of Rowcester and put a fake in its place to avoid detection of the crime. All had hoped their infuriated relations would buy them out, but as the hotel prospered, they had begun to enjoy the fruits of their labours. Then the hotel had burned down, Sir Philip had not paid the fire insurance, and although the Duke of Rowcester had married their partner, Harriet James, and had been generous in paying for the restoration of the hotel, they were once more in need of funds.

To stoop to crime in the days of their poverty, when all had a burning resentment at their humiliating treatment at the hands of their relatives was one thing; to turn to it again when they had known a certain amount of prosperity and success was another. But their joint ownership of the hotel, much as they grumbled about it, had become an obsession. The hotel must go on. And so Miss Tonks, the weakest, had been persuaded to go on a raiding mission to her sister, Mrs. Honoria Blessop, who was unaware that Miss Tonks had sunk to trade and still fondly imagined her living in one dingy London room.

Lady Fortescue owned the building. When Sir Philip had first suggested the hotel, the house in Bond Street had been all that Lady Fortescue possessed and she had lived

2

there alone with only her two old servants, John and Betty, for company.

Lady Fortescue, tall and white-haired, with snapping black eyes, surveyed the group. "I fear that sending Miss Tonks was not a good idea," she said. "She will return with some trifle which will not even pay a chambermaid's wages. Sir Philip, *you*, on the other hand, are accustomed to thieving."

"Let's see what Miss Tonks does," said Sir Philip. "I sometimes think the rest of you won't be happy until you see me dangling on the end of a rope."

"Have you ever thought it might be Miss Tonks who will end up dangling on the end of a rope?" asked the colonel.

"For pinching something from her own sister? Tcha!" said Sir Philip.

"We are fully booked for the Little Season." Mrs. Budley, her large pansy eyes looking around at the others, gave voice. She was in her early thirties but looked much younger with her cloud of soft brown hair and unlined face.

Lady Fortescue sighed. "But the Little Season is *cold*, and that means fires in all the rooms."

"Perhaps we should have approached the Duke of Rowcester?" suggested Mrs. Budley.

"My nephew and Harriet have gone abroad," said Lady Fortescue, "so that's out. I had thought of that already." She looked at the clock. "Dinner time, Colonel. Your arm, please."

Lady Fortescue and Colonel Sandhurst served the guests themselves in the dining-room, or rather, carried the first course to the tables, most of the work being done by two efficient waiters. But they knew their very presence in the dining-room gave the hotel cachet and put the prices up.

"Have you heard about Tupple's?" asked Sir Philip as they were on the point of leaving the room.

Lady Fortescue stopped. "You mean the new hotel over in George Street? No. But I gather it cannot compete with us. The food is reported to be dreadful."

"I saw Tupple himself skulking about our area steps," said Sir Philip. "He's probably after our cook."

"What, Despard? If he goes, we shall be ruined."

"You forget. He can't go," leered Sir Philip. "He's an escaped Frenchie off the hulks, ain't he? Wouldn't dare leave."

"You'd best have a word with him and remind him of that," said the colonel.

"Already have." Sir Philip grinned.

"To which he replied?" Lady Fortescue raised thin eyebrows.

"To which he replied that come the revolution, he would see my head in a basket first."

"Oh, dear!" Mrs. Budley opened her eyes to their widest in alarm. "Do you not think it rather dangerous to have such a bitter Frenchman in the kitchen?"

"Course it's dangerous," said Lady Fortescue. "But the man cooks like a genius. Our whole life is dangerous. If Miss Tonks gets into any trouble, we can't just sit here and let her take the blame herself."

"I can," said Sir Philip cheerfully. "I can just see her on the scaffold. All noble. As a farewell present, we'll buy her a white gown. She'd make a noble speech. Best moment in all her dreary life."

"You," said Lady Fortescue awfully, "are disgusting. Come, Colonel."

A look of hurt crossed Sir Philip's watery eyes. He saw Mrs. Budley looking at him reproachfully and defiantly poured himself a glass of port.

* * *

After a long journey in a comfortable post-chaise, Miss Tonks, after praying that something in the nature of highwaymen or thunderbolts would stop her inexorable journey into Gloucestershire, arrived unscathed at Chapping Manor, home of her sister, Honoria Blessop.

Chapping Manor had been the setting for many humiliations in Miss Tonks's dreary past. When her parents died, they had inexplicably left everything to Honoria, who gave a small yearly pittance to Miss Tonks. Not only that, but Mr. Blessop, Honoria's husband, had long ago seemed on the point of proposing marriage to Miss Tonks and then, inexplicably, he had veered off and married Honoria instead. Miss Tonks, on visits, was treated like the poor relation she was, being given sewing tasks and expected to take her meals on a tray in her room when Honoria was entertaining any distinguished company.

The slab-faced, over-corseted woman who was Honoria Blessop had produced two children, Cassandra and Edward. Edward had escaped from the maternal bosom to the navy. As she stood shivering on the steps of the manor, Miss Tonks calculated that Cassandra must be now eighteen. She had had one Season, that Miss Tonks knew from the social columns—*she* had not been invited to any of the functions during Cassandra's come-out—and had also heard through the grapevine that Cassandra had "not taken" and was still unwed.

The butler opened the door, saw Miss Tonks, and snapped his fingers at a footman to carry her modest trunk indoors.

"Are . . . are the family in the drawing-room, Brooks?" asked Miss Tonks timidly.

"Yes, Miss Letitia. You are to change and join them for dinner. We dine at six. Lord Eston is coming."

"Who is Lord Eston, Brooks?"

"His lordship is recently returned from the wars and lives at Courtfield Park not far from here, Miss Letitia."

"But why am I invited to sit down with them?" asked Miss Tonks. "You know I am not invited when grand company is expected."

"One of the ladies invited dropped out at the last minute," said Brooks. "May I point out, Miss Letitia, that you should go straight to your room. If you are found standing here talking to me, it would be frowned on."

"Oh, everything is frowned on," said Miss Tonks with a rare show of spirit. "Brooks, I am heartily sick of being frowned on."

The housekeeper, Mrs. Blodge, came crackling up. Her starched aprons always crackled.

"Your usual room is ready, Miss Letitia," she said. "Follow me."

Miss Tonks was led, not upstairs to the guest-rooms, but to an odd no man's land of a room in a stone passage leading to the servants quarters. It was barely furnished with an old iron bedstead, a toilet-table, and a thin rug on the stone floor. A great press large enough to house a whole family of skeletons took up one wall. No fire burnt in the grate. A tree tapped its branches mournfully against the one small dim window.

"I would like a fire," said Miss Tonks suddenly.

Mrs. Blodge folded her red hands across her ample stomach.

"You've never had a fire before, miss," she said.

"I am having one now," said Miss Tonks in a voice that trembled at her own temerity.

"Very good, Miss Letitia."

And that was that, thought Miss Tonks, as a footman appeared some moments later and began to build up a fire in the grate. Heavens, how brave of me! But if I am going to turn thief, I can surely be brave about little things.

She wondered whether to call for a maid to help her dress, but thought that might be going too far. She unpacked her belongings and laid them neatly in the huge press in the corner. On the bed, she spread out with loving hands a gold silk gown that Mrs. Budley had made for her. It was in quite the latest fashion. She sat down at the toilet-table and deftly set her mousy hair in something approaching a Roman style before slipping on that precious gown. Round her shoulders she spread a magnificent Paisley shawl, lent to her by Lady Fortescue, put some scent on a handkerchief, a present from the colonel, put a coral necklace, a present from Sir Philip, around her thin neck, and then drew on a pair of fine kid gloves, lent by Mrs. Budley. And so, feeling armoured by the donations of the other poor relations, she made her way to the drawing-room.

Honoria looked at her younger sister with eyes that bulged with surprise. How had Letitia come by that fashionable gown? And no one could ever in their wildest dreams have thought Letitia pretty, but there was something aristocratic about her long slender fingers and long narrow feet.

She pecked Miss Tonks on the cheek and murmured, "Don't go putting yourself forward. This is an important evening. Blessop and I have decided that Eston will do for Cassandra."

"Does Eston know of this?" asked Miss Tonks.

"How can he? He's not long arrived home."

"What is he like?"

"I don't know, you dithering fool. Never seen him."

"If you haven't seen him, how do you know he will do for Cassandra?" asked Miss Tonks.

"Because he's a lord, he's rich, and he owns Courtfield Park, and that should be enough for anyone. Now go and sit down."

Miss Tonks took a chair in a corner and surveyed the party. Cassandra Blessop came up to her and sat down beside her. "Just arrived, Aunt Letitia?"

"Yes, dear."

"Put you in solitary confinement, have they?"

"What?"

"That grubby little downstairs cell."

"Well, yes, my dear, but I am quite used to it. How pretty you look."

"No, I don't," said Cassandra. "And I look worse than usual tonight, do you not think?"

Miss Tonks could not help privately agreeing that the frilly pink muslin was the last thing Cassandra ought to be wearing. But she liked the girl's looks, although they were not fashionable. Cassandra had a plain, honest face with a dusting of golden freckles over a snub nose. She had flaming-red hair and hazel eyes and a generous mouth. Taken bit by bit, thought Miss Tonks, she was a social disaster. Red hair because of its association with the Scots was disliked, and her mouth was too large for beauty when little primped-up rosebud mouths were the fashion. But she glowed with warmth and colour, and Miss Tonks could only wonder, not for the first time, that her sister and her husband had managed to produce such a good-hearted and honest girl.

"This is all because of Lord Eston," said Cassandra. "If only he could turn out to be . . . well, ordinary, like me, someone friendly and not terrifying, then I could be at ease."

"Perhaps he is," said Miss Tonks. "You have no competition. I see your mama has not invited any other young person."

"No, and she's going to make it vulgarly clear to this Lord Eston that he's supposed to marry me, and even if I

8

looked like Venus that would be enough to make any man sheer off."

"There is always hope, Cassandra. Sometimes when I think I know what my life is going to be like, something very exciting happens."

Cassandra surveyed her aunt with interest. "I wouldn't have thought anything exciting would ever happen to you, Aunt Letitia," she said bluntly.

"Well, it has, and I shall tell you about it one day."

"Lord Eston," announced Brooks.

"Lor'," said Cassandra.

The guests had parted to either side of the room at his entrance and she had a full view of him.

He was slim and tall and handsome in a graceful way. He was impeccably tailored. His golden hair was teased and curled into the latest fashion. His blue eyes under heavy lids surveyed the room with an amused look.

Cassandra's lip curled. "A popinjay," she said.

"Cassandra!" came her mother's voice.

Cassandra slouched forward and stood awkwardly, looking at the carpet.

"Lord Eston, may I present my treasure, my Cassandra," said Honoria. "Curtsy to his lordship, Cassandra."

Cassandra gave a sort of bob.

The guests, who had been primed beforehand, moved off, as did Honoria, leaving the couple together.

"That's a very fine carpet," said Lord Eston.

"Is it?" mumbled Cassandra.

"Yes, you are looking at it so intently, I felt sure you must be admiring it as well."

"Come and meet my aunt," said Cassandra desperately. She walked away and he followed her to where Miss Tonks sat in the corner by the window.

"Aunt, this is Lord Eston," said Cassandra. "Lord Eston, Miss Tonks, my aunt."

Miss Tonks rose and curtsied. Cassandra made her escape.

Miss Tonks would, before her adventures with the poor relations, have been too timid to carry on any conversation with such an elegant gentleman, but work in the hotel, not to mention the evenings spent in the company of Sir Philip and the colonel, had given her an ease of manner she had not possessed before. To her surprise, she found she was telling him London gossip, unconsciously copying Lady Fortescue, who kept up with all the latest scandals, and Lord Eston suddenly laughed and said he thought she was a dangerous lady and Miss Tonks flushed with simple pleasure and said, "Oh, if only that were true. I should love to be a dangerous lady."

Honoria fumed as she watched them. She did not want to break up a conversation where her prize guest was so obviously being highly entertained, but after ten minutes, she decided enough was enough and propelled Cassandra towards Lord Eston by a series of sharp pushes in the back.

As Honoria approached, Miss Tonks fell silent, for the first time that evening taking in the full glory of the necklace her sister was wearing. It consisted of six strands of large diamonds, flashing and glittering in the light from the candelabra.

Miss Tonks blinked. That was it! That necklace! Oh, that would solve all their problems, and how very proud they would all be of her back at the Poor Relation. She barely heard dinner being announced.

Usually on previous visits, Miss Tonks had been too preoccupied with eating enough to bother much about anything else. But now she was used to good food and so was able to study Cassandra as she sat with her head bowed, replying in monosyllables to Lord Eston's gallant efforts at conversation.

Honoria weighed in, after casting a fulminating look at

her daughter, "Are you going to Mr. Hereford's hunt ball, Eston?" she asked.

"Yes, I shall be there."

"Then you must save a dance for my little Cassandra. She is simply pining to dance with you."

His blue eyes lit up with mocking laughter. "Now how can Miss Blessop pine for a dance with me when she has never met me before?"

"Ah, I know my little puss and I can see she is quite smitten."

"Mama!" whispered Cassandra in despair.

Lord Eston was suddenly sorry for her. "I shall be honoured to dance with Miss Blessop," he said.

"There was no need to be kind," said Cassandra when her mother's attention was elsewhere. "I think kindness can be a sort of insult,"

"Would you rather I was downright rude?" asked Lord Eston curiously. "Would you rather I said I would see you in hell first?"

Cassandra's eyes lit up with amusement for the first time that evening. "Something like that," she said, "then this sorry farce would be at an end. I think I would like to be a spinster like my Aunt Letitia."

"Why? Spinsters have a miserable time of it."

"So do wives," said Cassandra, "when they are forced to marry a man they do not like."

"Miss Blessop, I would never marry a lady who did not want me."

"Now how would you know?" asked Cassandra. "She could be threatened by her parents into *looking* as if she liked you."

"Miss Blessop, ladies swoon with delight when I approach them."

The hazel eyes studied his handsome face for a moment. "Yes, I suppose they would. You have a title and you are rich and you are not precisely an antidote."

"Alas, what can I say to move your heart?"

"Oh, tell the truth and admit you could not give a rap were my heart moved or not."

"When I first saw you, my blunt angel, in that . . . er . . . unfortunate pink gown, that might have been the case. But you see, I happen to find freckles very seductive."

Cassandra's hand flew to her nose. "Are they still there? Mama's maid has been bleaching them for *days*."

"Tell her to leave them alone."

"You know, you are making fun of me."

"In a way. You are so blunt. Cannot you flirt?"

"I am very bad at it."

His eyes caressed her. "I would teach you."

Cassandra shrank back in her chair. "Ah, you are determined to see if you can bring a blush to my cheek."

"Something like that. I apologize."

Old Sir Gerald Trust on Cassandra's other side claimed her attention and she turned away with relief, and to her mother's fury continued to talk to Sir Gerald for the rest of the meal.

Lord Eston found himself torn between pity for Cassandra and admiration, pity because she was forced to sing to him after dinner and she sang badly, admiration for her bluntness and honesty.

Miss Tonks sat making plans. No doubt Honoria would wear those diamonds to the Herefords' ball. Now the ball was in two days' time. She would watch and wait and as soon as those diamonds were taken out of Honoria's locked jewel box, she would dive into the room and steal them.

A shadow crossed her face. Honoria would immediately have the house searched. Miss Tonks's brow creased with worry. She could dart out and hide them in the

12

grounds. But then . . . but then . . . all the servants would fall under suspicion, and that could not be allowed to happen.

But all her moral scruples about stealing from her sister had vanished. For this had once been the family home. This drawing-room had been a pleasant welcoming place, not like it was now, new and glittering. Honoria had taken everything, as she always had, and put her stamp on it.

At least I didn't marry Edward Blessop, as I thought I might have done before Honoria took him away, thought Miss Tonks. I never thought he would turn out so weak and *rabbity,* but that is probably Honoria's doing. She drains the life out of everyone who comes near. Unless Cassandra escapes, she too will become dull and quiet.

The evening was at last at an end. Miss Tonks slipped away to her "cell," noticing with some surprise that the fire had been recently built up and was still burning brightly. She was just about to get ready for bed when Cassandra entered her room carrying a small pile of books. "Do you like novels, Aunt?" she asked. "This one is excellent. It is *Lady Penelope's Revenge.* Most exciting."

Miss Tonks took the volumes. "Well, it is most kind of you, my dear. I do not think I have ever read a novel before."

"Why not?"

"Your mother and I had a very strict governess who frowned on novels, and then, of course, when I came to live on my own in London, I had not . . . had not . . . the . . . er . . . time."

Miss Tonks had been about to say that she had not even had enough money to pay a subscription to a circulating library.

"I shall try these, dear," she went on. "What do you think of Lord Eston?"

Cassandra wrinkled her brow. "He is all very well, but

suitable for someone very fashionable and witty, I think. I would dearly like some man who would be a friend. But Mama will go on and on about Eston and so I have made up my mind. I shall give Eston the most horrible snub at the Herefords' ball, and then even Mama won't expect him to speak to me again."

"She will be absolutely furious," said Miss Tonks.

"I don't care. Eston don't want me, but he won't do anything to show it because . . . because I think he's kind, and so Mama will go on and go on pushing me in his direction unless I do something about it."

"You will be severely punished," said Miss Tonks.

"Pah. I have a good mind to run away and stay with you in that poky little room Mama says you have. But I must not stay talking to you, for if Mama finds me here, she will blame you for my bad behaviour. She always has to have someone to blame."

When she had left, Miss Tonks wearily sat down at the toilet-table and reached up to take the bone pins out of her hair. There came a scratching at the door and she heard her brother-in-law's voice say tentatively, "Letitia?"

"Come in," she said, turning about.

Mr. Edward Blessop sidled in. "Are you comfortable?" he asked.

"Yes, Edward. Thank you."

"Shouldn't put you in a room like this," he mumbled.

"I agree," said Miss Tonks. "But as you can see, I have a fire for the first time and that is extremely comfortable."

Edward gazed at the ceiling. "Thought you was looking extremely fine tonight."

"Thank you." Miss Tonks looked at him a trifle sadly. How she used to dream of him and long for the very sight of him. It all seemed very odd now.

"So all's right and tight, hey?"

"Yes, Edward."

"Going to the Herefords' ball?"

"Of course not. I have not been invited and you know very well Honoria would not dream of including me in the family party."

"You know, Letitia," he said in a rush, "you may think you are hard done by, you may think you have a poor time of it, but, demme, money isn't everything!" And with that, he scampered out of the room.

Poor man, thought Letitia, and yet he brought it on himself. Why did he tell me that? Was he trying to tell me he married Honoria for her money? And yet at that time, I fully expected both Honoria and myself to inherit equally.

She washed and undressed and climbed into the narrow hard bed and picked up the first volume of *Lady Penelope's Revenge* after adjusting a pair of spectacles on the end of her long thin nose.

The adventures of Lady Penelope seized Miss Tonks's attention by the throat, particularly the chapter where Lady Penelope dressed up as a highwayman in order to get those dreadful letters back from the wicked Count Orlando.

She finally fell asleep with a dreamy smile on her face, the candle beside the bed guttering in a pool of wax.

Miss Tonks awoke and blinked in surprise at the little maid who had set a cup of hot chocolate beside her bed and who was now drawing back the curtains. She had never been treated to such service before during her visits. The reason, although she did not know it, was that her adventures in London had given her a certain town bronze, which the servants, who were as snobbish as their masters, had recognized. So from being "poor old Miss Tonks" of previous visits, she had graduated to "that poor lady what doesn't deserve the treatment she gets."

So she sipped her chocolate gratefully and watched a footman come in with kindling and coals to make up the fire. She had nearly finished her chocolate when she was struck with the Great Idea. It came to her in a blinding flash. There was a way she could get those diamonds, a way that would not involve blame falling on the servants.

She would dress as a man, get a pistol from somewhere, hide in the bushes near the road on the eve of the ball and hold up her sister's coach!

∾∾∾∾∾∾∾∾∾∾∾∾∾∾∾∾∾∾

Chapter Two

Poverty is the mother of crime.
—MARCUS AURELIUS

CASSANDRA FOUND her aunt later that day in the morning-room, diligently cutting up old linen sheets and hemming them for handkerchiefs.

"Why do you not tell Mama you will not do such menial work?" demanded Cassandra.

"Because I should be sent packing," said Miss Tonks calmly, "and it suits me to stay. Tell me, Cassandra, how goes young Edward?"

"He appears to be leading an exciting life in the navy. Ah, that I were a man!"

"I suppose he took all his clothes with him."

Cassandra looked at her aunt in surprise. "Not all. There are some of his old duds left in his room. His shooting clothes, hunting clothes, things like that. Why do you ask?"

"I don't know," said Miss Tonks. "I often ask stupid questions."

Cassandra smiled at her and sat down next to her. "Give me a sheet. I may be a dreadful singer, but I am very good with a needle."

They stitched away in amicable silence until Cassandra said, "Does it not strike you as odd that your parents left all to my mother and virtually nothing to you?"

Miss Tonks sighed. "I have thought and thought about that. How could I have offended them?"

"Could it not be that they left all to Honoria as the elder but naturally expected her to look after you better?"

"I suppose it was something like that. Are you looking forward to the ball?"

"Of course not. It's all going to end up in the most frightful row."

"At what time do you set out?"

"Why?"

"I like to know things like that. Silly things."

"We are supposed to be there about nine, and so I suppose we will be there about nine-thirty so that we can make an entrance without being too vulgarly late. I shall actually be wearing a pretty dress, too, and not that pink fright."

"And your mama will be wearing her diamond necklace?"

"Not only that, Aunt Letitia, but her diamond tiara."

"Ouch!"

"Did you hurt yourself?"

"No," said Miss Tonks in a trembling voice. "The needle slipped." The tiara as well, she thought.

"Do you have many highwaymen or footpads around here?" asked Miss Tonks in what she hoped was a casual voice.

"No, it would be too hard for a villain to get away with anything. Everyone knows everyone else in the country."

"But surely with those diamonds, the coach should be guarded on the road to the Herefords."

"It is only a few miles to the Herefords and tomorrow is to be a full moon." Cassandra grinned. "I know what it is. It's Lady Penelope. You've got highwaymen on the brain."

"Perhaps." Miss Tonks stopped sewing and fixed a dreamy look on her face. "Did I ever tell you I was septic, Cassandra?"

"Heavens, have you the plague?"

Miss Tonks frowned. "Perhaps that is not the word. I know what is going to happen."

"Psychic. Or, as they would say in Scotland, the second sight. Dr. Johnson and Mr. Boswell travelled to the Hebrides to try to find proof of the second sight. Do you mean you can actually tell what is going to happen?"

"Not exactly." Miss Tonks primmed her lips and held a square of sheet up to the light to examine her stitching. "More a *feeling*. I keep seeing a highwayman." And that, thought Miss Tonks, might in a way buffer Cassandra from the shock of seeing her family held up.

Poor old thing. Got windmills in her cockloft, thought Cassandra inelegantly.

Later that day, when Cassandra had gone out on calls with her parents, Miss Tonks slipped quietly into young Edward's room holding a laundry bag. Into it she put a coat and breeches, stockings and square-toed shoes. In a press, she found a large slouched hat. Now all she had to do was hope the clothes fitted somehow and find a mask. She then raided Cassandra's room and discovered a black velvet mask and tucked that into the laundry bag as well.

She returned to her room. There was no key to the door, so she wedged a chair under the handle and tried on the clothes. They fitted her slim, flat-chested figure excellently, but they did more than that. She felt like another person, bold and strong and wicked. It was such a pity she could not have a horse. Even if she could get one from the stables, Mr. Blessop would be sure to recognize it. She undressed and put the clothes away and hid the bag under her mattress and then put on a warm cloak and went out, ostensibly for a walk but really to find the best place to lie in ambush.

She reached the end of the drive and then walked along a country road. There were high hedges on either side, rimed with frost. The day was very still and cold, and ice in the puddles cracked under the iron rings of the pattens on her feet.

The servants had told her that the Herefords' place lay west. Two miles from Chapping Manor, she found the exact spot. There was a bend in the road where the hedges on either side were extremely tall and thick, although devoid of leaves. She did a few practice stand-and-delivers until she felt as good an actress as Mrs. Siddons. Now back to the house to look for some sort of gun.

As in most country houses, there were guns all over the place, but Miss Tonks wanted something more portable than a fowling piece or blunderbuss. At last, in a drawer in the library, she found a box containing a pair of duelling pistols and took one. She had no intention of priming it. She could only hope that the sight of a masked man with a pistol would be enough.

Perhaps had it not been for *Lady Penelope's Revenge*, combined with her sister's more-than-usual crustiness and bad temper that evening, the spinster's heart would have failed her, but somehow taking the diamonds became as much a way of getting even with Honoria as keeping the hotel in funds, and before she fell asleep, there was the fantasy world of the novel to bolster her courage.

The day of the ball started quietly enough and then the house became a hive of activity as Honoria began her massive preparations.

Miss Tonks was instructed to take her evening meal on a tray in her room and she accepted the slight gladly. She kept glancing nervously at the chipped marble clock on the mantelpiece. The noise of its ticking seemed to become louder and louder as the moment for her to take action approached.

For one terrible moment, terror seized her by the throat as she fumbled her way into Edward Junior's clothes. But the minute they were on, she could feel that strange change of character coming over her again. She pulled the slouch hat down over her eyes, slipped the gun in one capacious pocket and the mask in another, opened the window, thankful for once that her room was on the ground floor, and slipped away through the glittering frost-covered shrubbery.

She made her way to the garden wall and climbed over, relishing the new freedom from corset and skirts. Even her walk had altered as she strode down the road. Miss Tonks was beginning to swagger.

She did, however, wish the moon were not so bright nor the frost so glittering. She felt as if she were walking across the centre of a stage.

But soon the road became dark as she reached the chosen stretch where tall hedges blotted out the moon. A fox slid across the road, making her jump. She climbed up the bank and stood in the shadow of the hedgerow and waited.

Cassandra, almost pretty in a gown of white muslin edged with a gold key pattern and with white silk flowers in her flaming hair, waited impatiently for her mother.

But Honoria Blessop was battling with a "divorce" corset, that latest of corsets which actually separated the breasts. She would not believe it was too small for her, would not believe that she had put on weight since it had been sent down from London two months ago, and so three maids pulled and pushed and sweated to try to get her folds of flesh into it.

Cassandra decided to go and show her Aunt Letitia her new gown. But when she pushed open the door of Miss Tonks's room, there was no one there. Miss Tonks's gown that she had been wearing that day was flung across the bed, as was her petticoat and corset. Deciding at last that her aunt had changed into something else, Cassandra searched the house and then asked the servants, but no one had seen Miss Tonks.

Miss Tonks was jolted out of her dreams by the sound of jingling harness in the distance and the thud of iron-shod hooves on the frosty road. She said a hurried little prayer and went and stood in the middle of the road, slipped on her mask and held the duelling pistol out in front of her with both hands.

She had chosen her place so that the carriage would turn the bend of the road and see her, but leaving enough of a straight stretch between her and the bend for the coachman to stop his horses.

The coach was very near now. The glitter of a carriage lamp bobbed round the corner like a searching eye.

Miss Tonks closed her eyes and held out the duelling pistol in a firmer grip and shouted, "Stand and deliver!"

"Whoa!" shouted a masculine voice. Horses plunged and then horses were still.

"Stand and deliver!" shouted Miss Tonks again.

"Do you know," said a lazy voice, "I don't think I will."

Miss Tonks's eyes flew open. She let out a gasp and then sat down in the road and burst into tears. For facing her in a racing curricle and holding a long pistol was Lord Eston.

Lord Eston climbed down and unhitched a lantern

from the side of his curricle and approached the sobbing figure. He stooped and took the pistol out of his assailant's nerveless hand and then untied the strings of the mask. The blotched and tearful face of Miss Letitia Tonks looked up at him.

"Playing games, Miss Tonks?" he asked.

All Miss Tonks had to say was that it had all been a silly joke, but she saw the scaffold at Newgate rearing up above her and heard the jeering of the bloodthirsty crowd. She gasped and hiccuped. "It was not you I meant to rob, my lord, but my sister."

"Why?"

"Because I wanted her diamonds. I need the money. Oh, it will all come out at my trial. I am part owner of the hotel the Poor Relation, only Honoria does not know that. We are in need of funds and I told the others I would go to my sister's and steal something. Oh, oh, oh!"

He seized her by the elbow and pulled her up. He guided her to his curricle and told her to climb up. Then he jumped in beside her and picked up the reins and urged his team forward. He drove a little way until he saw a farm gate by the side of the road. He opened it and led his horses and carriage through and round until they were hidden from the road by the hedge and then returned and closed the gate again.

"Give me your hat," he said.

Sniffling miserably, Miss Tonks pulled it off. He put on her mask and pulled her hat down over his eyes and buttoned his long greatcoat up to the neck. Miss Tonks gazed at him bleakly, too frightened now to cry. She thought he was going to execute her there in the field.

His next words startled her. "Now, sit here, Miss Tonks, and pull a carriage rug about you and I will show you how it should be done. Are you sure they will come this way?"

"They have to," said Miss Tonks. "But . . ."

"Don't make a fuss." His eyes glinted with amusement in the moonlight.

He vaulted over the farm gate and strode down to where he had come across Miss Tonks. He felt amusement bubbling up inside him. Honoria Blessop was such a monumental horror, she deserved to lose her diamonds.

He heard the coach approaching and moved closer to the shadow of the hedge. He did not want to emulate Miss Tonks's mistake by holding up the wrong coach.

"And you will behave prettily to Lord Eston," Honoria Blessop was saying to her daughter. "He is a great catch and we mean to secure him before he reaches those harpies in London. Remember, you cost us a great deal of money with that Season. It is your duty to repay us."

"Mama," said Cassandra, "why is it that you are so rich and Aunt Letitia is so poor?"

"Because that's the way God ordained it," said Honoria. "Everything that happens is the hand of God."

The coach lurched to a stop. "Stand and deliver!" shouted a gruff voice.

"My diamonds, oh, my daughter, oh, my diamonds," shouted Honoria like some sort of female Shylock. "Get down from the box," they heard that same terrible voice ordering the coachman, "and you too," to the groom at the back.

It flashed through Cassandra's frightened mind that Aunt Letitia must really have the second sight. Then the carriage door was opened and a tall figure ordered them all out.

"Those diamonds," barked the highwayman. "Put them on the ground."

"No," shrieked Honoria.

He raised the pistol and balanced it across his arm and took aim.

"Take them off, you silly woman," shouted Edward Blessop."

Cassandra faced the highwayman. "Will you go away and leave us unharmed if we give you the jewels?"

He smiled. "Yes."

She unfastened the necklace from around her mother's neck and flung it on the ground and then lifted off the tiara and dropped it beside the necklace. Honoria was making gasping and moaning noises.

"Into the coach," ordered the highwayman. "You"—he pointed the pistol at Cassandra—"stay where you are."

Any doubts he had had about thieving the jewels from Mrs. Blessop disappeared when he noticed how she dived into the shelter of the coach, followed by her husband, neither of them making a stand to protect their daughter.

Cassandra drew off the pearl ring she was wearing and threw it at him. "This is all I have," she said contemptuously.

He thrust the pistol in his pocket and seized her in his arms. "You have other treasures," he murmured, and his mouth came down on her own. Shock kept her still in his arms. And then he released her and, scooping up the jewels, moved quickly up the road until he was lost to view. Cassandra stared after him in a dazed way. Then she picked up her pearl ring, which he had left lying on the ground. Through all her confusion and fright came the one clear thought: Mama will not expect us to go to the ball now.

But her mother had recovered now that she was safe and was in a blazing temper. Cassandra noticed that she did not pause in her tirade to ask if her daughter was unharmed. "We are going to the Herefords," she shouted. "Yes! For they can send out the militia."

"My dear," said her husband. "What is this? Poor Cassandra has been frightened out of her wits and we are in no fit state to—"

"We go," said Honoria, now icily calm. "And Cassandra will see that she charms Lord Eston."

Now was the time to warn her mother that she had every intention of giving Lord Eston a disgust of her, but Cassandra was still too numb and shocked to make any sound.

Miss Tonks looked in awe at the sparkling diamonds in her lap. "I do not know how to thank you, Lord Eston," she whispered. "But I feel guilty. I have involved you in crime."

"I involved myself," he said. "Now I must go to the ball. You cannot walk down the road carrying those diamonds. Here! Wrap them in this rug."

"You are a hero," said Miss Tonks, gazing up at him. "I shall never tell anyone what you have done. No, not if they drag me and whip me at the cart's tail."

Lord Eston bit back a smile. He felt sure that the customary punishment for prostitutes would never fall on Miss Tonks's thin shoulders.

"Tell me," he asked curiously, "are you all such practised villains at that hotel that you will be able to sell these valuable gems and not be discovered?"

"Oh, we shall break them up into single gems or get them reset," said Miss Tonks blithely. "But we are all very respectable, I assure you. It was being poor relations that drove us to such straits. You have no idea of the petty humiliations to which one is subject. So much more worthy to be in trade."

"I agree. But stealing is hardly being in trade."

Miss Tonks looked miserable and then brightened. "But we shall only be *borrowing* the value of the diamonds, you see. As soon as we are in profit, we shall send Honoria the money anonymously and she can buy more. As a matter of fact, she is so very rich, she could buy more tomorrow. Oh, since you have done me such a very great service, I feel I should warn you."

"Of what?"

"Poor Cassandra is being bullied into setting her cap at you. She has decided to put an end to matters by being very rude to you at the ball. Please do not think badly of her."

He raised her hand to his lips and kissed it. "I shall not even blush. Off with you, Miss Tonks. You are a very wicked woman."

He went to the gate and looked up and down the road before opening it for her. With the diamonds muffled in a large bearskin rug, and the duelling pistol she had borrowed safely back in her pocket, Miss Tonks whispered a farewell and marched off down the road.

She felt very elated and brave. Already she was rehearsing how she would tell the others of how she had turned highwayman, and of course as she had to protect Lord Eston's good name, they would never know she had not committed the robbery herself.

Honoria Blessop created a sensation on arrival at the Herefords by standing at the entrance to the ballroom and shouting, "I have been robbed by a highwayman!"

Then she manufactured a swoon, collapsing into her husband's arms, who tottered under her weight. Mr. Hereford sent servants off to alert the parish constable and to call out the militia. Only when Honoria heard Mr. Blessop being urged to take his family home did she pretend to rally, saying that her darling Cassandra must enjoy the ball. No highwayman should be allowed to spoil her daughter's evening. Cassandra found it all very embarrassing and could only be glad that Lord Eston had not put in an appearance. But no sooner had all the inquiries as to details of the highwayman's appearance been dealt with, no sooner was she seated beside her mother, than Lord Eston appeared.

Mr. Hereford spoke to him. He looked across at Honoria and her daughter and then crossed the ballroom floor towards them. "Smile!" hissed Honoria. "Here he comes."

Cassandra scowled dreadfully.

"I am shocked to learn you have been robbed, Mrs. Blessop," said Lord Eston. "You must have been dreadfully frightened. Should you not be at home?"

"Alas, my lord," said Honoria, "my puss here was so determined to dance with you that nothing would prevent her from coming."

"I trust the highwayman did not harm you in any way?" he asked Cassandra.

"He kissed me," said Cassandra.

"He *what*?" shrieked her mother. "You did not tell me that!"

Cassandra looked at her with cold eyes. "And yet you and Papa went back into the carriage and left me with him and did not think to ask me if anything had occurred."

"How dreadful for you," said Lord Eston.

"As a matter of fact, it was quite pleasant."

"Cassandra!" wailed Honoria, but there was worse to come.

"May I have this dance, Miss Blessop?" asked Lord Eston, his eyes dancing.

"No, you may not," said Cassandra. "I do not want to dance with you, now or at any other time."

"You have broken my heart," he said solemnly and turned and walked away.

Honoria sat stricken. Her husband had gone into the card-room. She must go and get him and tell him to take them home, but she felt her legs would not move.

"Where's that sister of yours?" demanded a dowager on her other side. "Heard she was staying with you."

"Letitia is well, I thank you," said Honoria, her great shock at Cassandra's behaviour being replaced by white rage.

"Brave of you to give her house room," said the dowager, "and tactful of you not to bring her here."

"What are you talking about?" demanded Honoria shrilly, giving the dowager her whole attention for the first time.

"Well, she's sunk to trade, ain't she?"

"Explain yourself."

"Partner in that hotel in Bond Street, the Poor Relation, that's what she is."

Honoria's face cleared. "You are mistaken. I called at the hotel myself and the Miss Tonks who is a partner there is a frightful old woman." Honoria had in fact met Sir Philip in a cap and gown masquerading as Miss Tonks.

"No, no," cackled the dowager. "Ask Hereford. He and Mrs. Hereford dined with the Rochesters there last year. Miss Tonks was acting as a sort of chambermaid, so Rochester said."

Enough was enough. Outrage gave Honoria strength to move. "Come," she said, taking Cassandra's arm in a strong grip, rising and then marching her like a jailer to the door. "Mr. Hereford," she said, "we are after all a trifle too shaken to stay. Please have our carriage brought round and my husband summoned from the card-room."

She maintained a grim silence until they were all seated in the carriage and then she began to rant and rave. Cassandra herself was now horrified at the enormity of what she had done, but she sat with her lips folded in a firm line and said not a word. "And there is worse," went on Honoria to her husband. "Letitia is in *trade*. She hoodwinked us. She is in fact working in that disgraceful hotel. No, no, that must have been someone masquerading as her we met. But

I shall get my revenge. I am throwing her out this night and she can *walk* to the nearest inn for shelter."

"It is very cold," volunteered Edward timidly.

"I don't care if she freezes to death. And as for you, miss, you will go away as well. Yes, I know what to do with you. There is a seminary in Bath run on very strict lines for wayward females. By the end of this week, I shall take you there."

Cassandra felt weak tears rising in her eyes. She wished with all her heart that the highwayman would hold them up again and take her away.

Miss Tonks heard the carriage arriving and assumed that the shock of the robbery had made her sister forgo the ball. She settled down to finish *Lady Penelope's Revenge*.

Her first thought when Honoria burst into the room was gratitude that the diamonds were safely hidden, as were the men's clothes she had used for the masquerade, and that the duelling pistol was safely back in its box with its fellow.

"You," said Honoria, pointing at her, "have sunk so low that I heard a report this night that you were working as a chambermaid."

Miss Tonks gave a weak laugh. "What nonsense."

"Are you or are you not a partner in that hotel in Bond Street?"

Miss Tonks took a deep breath. "Yes," she said.

"How dare you stoop so low!"

"I was nigh starving," said Miss Tonks.

"Fiddle. Get out of my house this moment, you slut. You can walk to the nearest inn."

"Very well," said Miss Tonks with a calmness she did not feel, for she was wondering how she could manage to walk the miles to the nearest inn on a freezing night carrying her trunk.

"It is your malign influence in this house that made my Cassandra behave so dreadfully tonight," Honoria went on. "I was held up by a brute of a highwayman who stole my diamonds, and Cassandra had the temerity to tell Lord Eston—Lord Eston!—that the highwayman had kissed her and she liked it. Then she said she did not want to dance with him. She will go to a seminary in Bath and have the nonsense whipped out of her."

"You," said Miss Tonks in a trembling voice, "are a low, horrible, vulgar woman who kept me on such short commons that I had to sink to trade . . . no, not *sink* . . . to elevate myself to become partner in a successful venture. At least have the decency to get out and leave me in peace to pack!"

The slamming of the door answered her.

Miss Tonks rose and dressed. She felt cold and calm and brave. She had the diamonds and her friends would be proud of her. She dressed in a wool gown and warm cloak after packing the diamond tiara and necklace at the foot of her trunk. She looked ruefully at the bearskin carriage rug belonging to Lord Eston. She would need to throw it away out on the road, or better, hide it in some field. It was too bulky to go in her trunk. She could not leave it behind to cause inquiries as to where it had come from.

Perhaps Cassandra's adventures would have ended in a seminary in Bath if Miss Tonks had not decided to stay her departure until she had finished *Lady Penelope's Revenge*. She had just reached the last chapter of the last volume when her door opened and Cassandra slipped in. Her face was blotched with weeping.

"Sit down by the fire, my dear," said Miss Tonks. "This is a sad business. Could you not tell your mama that you were so overset by the highwayman that you were rude to Lord Eston?"

Cassandra shook her head. "I have decided to come with you, Aunt, if you will have me."

31

"Of course I will, and gladly. But I shall be accused of kidnapping or something."

"Not if I leave a letter."

"But it is so cold and such a long walk to the nearest inn, for Honoria is not letting me have a carriage."

"As to that," said Cassandra, "the coachman, Philip, will do anything I ask. I shall slip over to the stables and ask him to help us and then pack a few things. Shall I work in the hotel with you? I shall not need pretty ballgowns for that."

"We now have servants in the hotel." Miss Tonks thought quickly. In order to have more rooms for guests in the newly refurbished hotel, the poor relations had taken an apartment next door for their sleeping quarters. There was a spare little room next to her own. That would do very well for Cassandra.

"My dear," she said earnestly, "much as I would love your company, please think carefully of what you are doing. You are ruining all chance of making a good marriage, possibly of any marriage at all."

"Good," said Cassandra fiercely. "Now I will go and rouse Philip."

"I would have thought Honoria would have locked you in your room."

Cassandra grinned like a schoolboy and held up a ring of keys. "I have been locked in so many times in disgrace that I had these keys copied."

Soon she and Miss Tonks were jogging along in the second-best carriage under the burning stars.

"It was very bold of you," said Miss Tonks, "to tell Lord Eston that you had liked the highwayman's kiss. Do you not think, my dear, that Lord Eston might be able to kiss you like that?"

"Pooh! Men like Lord Eston are made by their tailor. But is it not marvellous that you really do have the gift of

32

the second sight? You saw a highwayman and a highway-man appeared!"

Miss Tonks was almost tempted to tell her about the diamonds, to tell her that the highwayman and Lord Eston were one and the same. But just in case she was ever discovered guilty of the theft, then there must be nothing to implicate Cassandra.

Lord Eston called at Chapping Manor the following after-noon, ostensibly to pay his respects to Mr. and Mrs. Blessop but in fact to find out how Miss Tonks had fared and if she had the diamonds well hidden. Also, it would be amusing to tease Cassandra a little. She deserved it for being so rude.

After being kept waiting for a full quarter of an hour, the butler told him in a hollow voice that Mrs. Blessop would receive him in the drawing-room. Lord Eston began to feel guilty. The house was so dark and still and quiet, as if someone had died. He hoped he had not shocked Cassandra so much in his highwayman's guise that she had gone into a decline. He had an aunt who went into a decline if she saw a mouse.

Mrs. Blessop was alone in the drawing-room. He felt disappointed.

"My compliments, ma'am," he said, bowing low. "I trust you have recovered from your ordeal?"

"Thank you, but I fear my nerves are very delicate."

"Is Mr. Blessop at home?"

"He has gone out hunting."

"Miss Blessop is well?"

"Yes, my lord, although I fear her sensibilities were so shattered by that highwayman that she was rude to you." Honoria had no intention of even hinting that her daughter had left with Miss Tonks.

"All is forgiven," he said with a smile. "I should very much like to pay my respects to Miss Blessop."

"Alas, she is lying down with the headache."

This was said in a very grim voice so that Lord Eston began to wonder whether Mrs. Blessop was beginning to suspect he had been the highwayman. She did not offer him any refreshment, so after a few more courtesies he took his leave, feeling very disappointed.

He drove slowly along the road, remembering how Miss Tonks had tried to hold him up. What a dreary day it was, with a leaden sky threatening snow and a chill wind whistling through the hedges on either side with a thin keening note.

And then, as he approached the farm gate he had opened the night before, he heard a high voice singing drunkenly, "Tol rol, diddle dol."

He stopped his carriage and jumped lightly down, tethering his horses to the gatepost. He vaulted over the gate and looked around.

Exactly where he and Miss Tonks had hidden the night before lay Edward Blessop on the frosty ground, a bottle in one hand and singing tunelessly.

"Good day, Mr. Blessop," said Lord Eston. "No sport?"

"Lost 'em all," said Edward, waving the bottle. "All gone. All the pretty birds flown."

"You lost the hunt?"

"Lost, lost, lost. Letitia lost, Cassandra lost. All gone."

Lord Eston crouched down beside him. "Where's your mount?"

"All gone," said Edward, looking at him stupidly. "Threw me in the six acre and trotted back to his stable. Gone, gone, gone."

"I had better take you home, old man, or you will die with the cold. What will that pretty daughter of yours think if she sees you in this state?"

"All gone. Gone with Letitia. Gone in the night.

Flown the coop," said Edward as Lord Eston helped him to his feet.

"Do you mean your daughter has left with Miss Tonks?" demanded Lord Eston sharply. "No, throw the bottle away, there's a good chap."

"Shan't," said Edward. He took a swig out of it. "Whassat? Cassandra? Little Cassandra's gone to that hotel. Ruined forever. Gone."

"I have my carriage. Now through the gate we go," said Lord Eston, propelling Edward. "Up you go. But you really should get rid of that bottle before your wife sees you."

"Don't care," said Edward and then giggled and hiccuped.

He was fast asleep when Lord Eston reached Chapping Manor, so he told the anxious servants that their master had taken a toss on the hunting field and should be carried to bed without disturbing Mrs. Blessop.

Then he drove off in a high good humour. So little Cassandra had gone to the Poor Relation Hotel with her aunt!

How dark and cold the country was in winter. The lights of London beckoned—and a warm sweet pair of lips and a snub nose covered in freckles. He began to whistle as he went home to pack.

Chapter Three

Many speak the truth when they say that
they despise riches, but they mean the riches
possessed by other men.

—CHARLES CALEB COLTON

"I WONDER what that wretched woman is up to?" demanded Lady Fortescue.

"By which you mean Miss Tonks?" Sir Philip looked bored at the very idea of discussing the spinster.

"I wish you would not call her 'that wretched woman,'" said Mrs. Budley with a rare show of spirit. "How we could ever have expected such a genteel lady to turn to crime is beyond me. The hotel is nearly full. We could, perhaps, be a trifle more vulgarly pressing as to the quick settlement of bills and then we could remain honest."

Colonel Sandhurst heaved a heavy sigh. "When did the aristocracy ever settle their bills promptly? They delight in not settling them at all."

The owners of the Poor Relation were in their sitting-room, formerly a schoolroom at the top of the house, which had been restored after the fire. They retired there late in the evening after dinner for conversation and tea served to them by Lady Fortescue's old servants, Betty and John.

"My apologies, Mrs. Budley," said Lady Fortescue, "but fear for Miss Tonks has made me a trifle acid about her. Such ladies of timid disposition have a craving to be found out. She will take some insignificant trifle which could not possibly keep us in candles for a week and be caught in the act."

Sir Philip threw her a malicious look. "So ladies of timid disposition like to get found out, do they? Was that why your nephew, the Duke of Rowcester, caught you with those silver candlesticks?"

"Really, sir!" barked the colonel.

"I was unlucky," said Lady Fortescue evenly. "How was I to know Rowcester would notice those candlesticks were missing? And while we're on the subject, you never yet told us what it was you took from him."

Sir Philip sat very still, like a lizard on a rock, staring at her unblinkingly. That gem-studded barbaric necklace he had stolen from the duke had been replaced by a clever fake. He had no intention of telling the others what it was he had stolen. But somehow he intended to buy it back from the villainous jeweller he had taken it to and to whom he was paying a small sum from time to time to keep the necklace unbroken and unsold.

"It is better you do not know," he said sanctimoniously. "I am prepared to carry the blame if we are found out."

Colonel Sandhurst's blue eyes rested thoughtfully on Sir Philip. "That's a noble thought," he said. "And I don't know why it is that the sound of you being noble makes me uneasy, but it does. We must all decide to be very kind to Miss Tonks. She will no doubt return to us empty-handed, and I for one hope she does."

Lady Fortescue's black eyes turned on him. "If you are so concerned for Miss Tonks's welfare, perhaps you should marry her."

"Perhaps I should," retorted the colonel, and he and Lady Fortescue glared at each other.

Mrs. Budley stared at them in distress. They must both surely be in their seventies, a great age, and yet they fenced like lovers, and any time things looked like settling down between them was the time that the equally elderly Sir Philip would decide to flirt with Lady Fortescue, the jealous colonel would turn tetchy, and another row would erupt.

But she said aloud, "I wonder what Miss Tonks is doing now?"

"Probably cringing in some corner of her sister's drawing-room, mending clothes, and praying for a miracle," said Sir Philip.

Miss Tonks was, in fact, preparing for bed in a pretty room in an inn on the second night of their journey to London. Cassandra, she knew, was beginning to feel depressed, all the euphoria of escaping from home seeping away.

Using the bed curtains as a screen, Miss Tonks stripped down to her shift and then realized that she had not unpacked her night-gown and let out an exclamation of annoyance.

"What is the matter?" called Cassandra.

"I have forgot to unpack my night-rail."

"I'll get it for you."

"Thank you, my dear." And then she had a sudden picture of those jewels lying at the bottom of her trunk and cried, "No!" and shot round the bed and stood protectively over her belongings.

"I will get it myself," she said. "Please go to bed."

She looked so frightened and shaken, standing there in nothing but her shift, that Cassandra wondered what it was that Aunt Letitia had in the trunk that she did not want her to see. Probably a miniature of an old love or something like that, thought Cassandra.

She climbed into bed. Miss Tonks had covered the foot of it with the large bearskin rug which she had carried with her since they had left Chapping Manor.

Cassandra waited until Miss Tonks had climbed in beside her and then said, "This is a fine rug, but a trifle cumbersome. Do you always take it with you?"

"Oh, always," said Miss Tonks firmly. "I never travel without it. Carriages can be so draughty. I hope you are not too worried about your parents."

"I confess I am sorry to have hurt Papa, for he is always kind. But Mama must be shocked into seeing sense. I have no wish to marry. Tell me more about these people with whom you work. Will they like me? Will I like them? Will they accept me?"

"So many questions," sighed Miss Tonks, snuggling down under the blankets. "Well, I suppose the leader of our little family must be Lady Fortescue. She is very old indeed but tall and straight with white hair and the most piercing black eyes. Next comes Colonel Sandhurst, equally old. Such a fine figure of a man despite his age! Always impeccably dressed and a true gentleman. He has thick white hair and blue eyes and a kind face. Then," went on Miss Tonks, her voice sharpening perceptibly, "there is Sir Philip Somerville. He is a nasty wizened creature, quite spiteful, and he often smells. Ladies are not supposed to notice when a gentleman smells, but he does use too much scent."

"Why do you tolerate him?"

"To be fair, if there are difficulties with the guests in the hotel, he is the one who always copes admirably with the situation. Pay him no heed. He will not trouble you. He reserves his malice for me."

"Anyone else?"

"Mrs. Budley, who is all that is pretty and charming and a very great friend. I am indeed fortunate. Cassandra, I hope I have not helped you to wreck your life. By this move you have put yourself beyond the pale. No gentleman will want to marry you."

"I do not care for *gentlemen*," said Cassandra. "There are other men in the world."

Miss Tonks stiffened like a board. "You cannot possibly marry below your rank."

"Why not?"

"Because people of low rank do not share our finer feelings and sensitivities."

"Aunt Letitia, I cannot believe that to be true. I have observed that servants have the same feelings as we have."

But Miss Tonks's mind could not accept this heresy. Why else had she eked out a miserable penurious existence for all those years instead of finding work? Everyone knew God punished those who moved out of their appointed stations in life. Although she was in trade, her partners were not of the ungenteel.

"Try to go to sleep," she said instead. "We will be in London tomorrow evening."

But Cassandra lay awake, listening to the bustle of coaches arriving and coaches departing in the inn yard below. The inn was situated on the main Oxford road and so it resounded with perpetual stir and bustle: doors opening and shutting, bells ringing, voices calling to the waiter from every quarter, while he cried "Coming" to one room while hurrying off to another. Everyone seemed to be in a hurry, either arriving and impatient to be indoors, or rushing to depart homewards. Every now and then a carriage rattled up to the main entrance with a rapidity that shook the house. The man who cleaned the boots was running in one direction, the barber with his powder bag in the other, then the barber's boy with his hot water and razors, followed by the clumping feet of the washerwoman delivering clean laundry. A horn blew sharply to announce the arrival of the post.

Did these servants never sleep, thought Cassandra, and would she herself be expected to be on duty at the hotel day and night? Or were hotels more genteel and was there a period during the night when the guests were expected to sleep?

She thought of the highwayman again and felt his mouth against her own. He had been clean-shaven, and his lips, warm and sweet. But behind the mask, he was probably ugly and brutal-looking. Silly to dream of him. Silly to hope he would arrive again in her life one day and carry her off. But then what would her life be like? Consorting with criminals and their doxies in hedge taverns, fearing all the time that the Runners might arrive? If only life were like life in romances! Ah, then the highwayman would sell the jewels, become a gentleman and go in search of her. Cassandra stifled a giggle. And he would find her working in an hotel and think her *far* too much beneath him.

A stab of guilt about her parents went through her but she consoled herself with the thought that both knew where to find her. It was not as if she had run away and not told them where she was going. And here she was with her respectable aunt.

Beside her, Miss Tonks, too, lay awake. She tried to imagine what the jewels would fetch. Then she thought it such a pity that poor Cassandra in the first flush of youth should have to put romance behind her. Now if there was a way to bring her out at the Season, that would solve all the problems. Perhaps some man would love her so much that he would not mind the fact that she had run away from her family to live in an hotel. Her thoughts turned to Lord Eston. He had been so very kind and not at all shocked at the idea of holding up Honoria and taking her jewels. But young men were notoriously wild. He probably thought it no end of a joke. No, such as Lord Eston would not do.

The morning was bitter cold and snow was beginning to fall as Cassandra and Miss Tonks climbed into a post-chaise, the Blessop family carriage having been sent back as soon as they had been deposited at the local inn. Miss Tonks settled the bearskin rug over their knees. She would send it back to Lord Eston with a note of thanks. One gloved hand stroked the fur. Of course, she could always sell it. Lord Eston was very rich and probably travelled with a whole carriageful of dead animal skins.

"I hope we reach London before the snow gets too heavy," said Cassandra as they moved off with that irritating jerk always inflicted on passengers by the drivers of post-chaises. Why did it happen? Did they startle the horses so that they leapt forward in the traces? Cassandra tried to keep her mind on such trivia to stop herself worrying about the immediate future. The other "poor relations" did not know of her imminent arrival. What if they sent her packing?

Snow was twisting and swirling outside, falling between the upraised skeletal arms of the winter trees. Thicker and thicker it fell as the carriage bumped along over ruts and holes in the road. All heat had gone from the bricks at their feet, and despite the heavy bearskin both began to shiver.

"We cannot go on," said Miss Tonks. "We must find somewhere to stop."

As if the driver had had the same thought, the post-chaise crawled under an arch and into the courtyard of a posting-house. Miss Tonks rubbed the steam from the glass and peered out nervously. "It looks *very* expensive," she said, fumbling in her reticule. "I do not know . . ."

"I have money with me," said Cassandra.

Stiff with cold, both women alighted. But in the hall of the posting-house, they were met by the owner, Mr. Box, a tall, thin man with an expression of glacial snobbery. He surveyed the shivering pair and informed them that he had no rooms left.

"But you must have," exclaimed Cassandra. Miss Tonks stood silently, hanging her head. The brave woman who had attempted to hold up a coach had gone, to be replaced by a spinster used to a life of cruel snubs.

"There is quait a comfortable inn half a mile along the road with modest prices," said Mr. Box.

"Meaning that we cannot afford your prices, you popinjay," exclaimed Cassandra furiously.

Lord Eston stood in the doorway in his many-caped greatcoat and raised his quizzing-glass. What other female in the whole of England had that blunt manner?

The owner of the posting-house saw the magnificent figure that was Lord Eston and rushed forward, contemptuously brushing past Miss Tonks as he did so. He bowed so low that his nose nearly touched the ground. "At your service, my lord," he said, recognizing Lord Eston from previous visits that gentleman had made to the posting-house on his road to London. "Charles will take your lordship's traps to his room."

"A moment, if you please," said Lord Eston. "I believe I espy two dear friends." He walked forward. "Why, it is Miss Tonks and Miss Cassandra! Ladies, I am overjoyed. But why are you standing here like waifs next to your trunks?" He swung round and stared awfully at the owner.

"Fan me ye winds!" exclaimed Mr. Box, striking his forehead in a theatrical gesture. "I had quite forgot. We have a very good bedchamber available and the ladies are most welcome to it."

"I don't want it now," said Cassandra. "Let us go."

"Stay, Miss Cassandra," urged Lord Eston. "Only

mark how poor Miss Tonks shivers so. You would not get very far in this dreadful weather."

"Indeed! But this person has assured us that there is another inn close by with *modest* prices."

"I would admire your determination for revenge at any other time." Lord Eston looked down at her with affectionate amusement. "But you must not stand on your dignity in a snowstorm when the only alternative is an inn with bad food and worse beds."

"Please let us stay here," murmured Miss Tonks. "We need the protection of a gentleman. Ladies travelling alone are often subject to insult."

Cassandra looked at Miss Tonks's miserable face and capitulated.

"Very well," she said stiffly. "Have our trunks carried upstairs."

"I would be honoured if you would both join me for dinner." Lord Eston smiled at Cassandra, who suddenly appeared to find the posting-house carpet every bit as fascinating as she had found the drawing-room carpet of her home when Lord Eston had first spoken to her.

"It will be laid for your lordship in a private parlour at four o'clock," said Mr. Box.

"Oh, really!" Cassandra's eyes flashed with contempt. "First there is no room, and now suddenly *two* bedchambers and a private parlour are available."

"Cassandra," said Miss Tonks miserably, "don't *squabble*. My lord, we are honoured to accept your invitation."

They were led upstairs to a charming bedchamber on the first floor overlooking the garden at the back. "Now this is more like it!" Miss Tonks spread her thin hands out in front of the fire. "Such a coincidence, Eston arriving when he did. And you must admit, Cassandra, it is handsome of him to offer to entertain us after you had snubbed him so dreadfully."

"I amuse him for the moment," retorted Cassandra. "Such as Lord Eston will do anything to be amused."

Miss Tonks thought of Lord Eston cheerfully volunteering to hold up the coach and gave a shiver. For one brief moment, when she had noticed how affectionately he had looked at Cassandra, she had begun to hope that, after all, here might be the man for her, a man who would not be put off by the fact she had run away from home to work in an hotel. But she had to admit to the good sense of what Cassandra had said and so never noticed that Cassandra was spreading out a very pretty gown of thin muslin ready to put on, nor did she realize that a young lady who absolutely detested Lord Eston would hardly consider wearing thin muslin on such a day.

By the time they sat down at the dinner table in Lord Eston's private parlour, both were very hungry, having only eaten some thin toast that morning. Cassandra in her white muslin gown with a scarlet-and-gold Paisley shawl draped over her shoulders looked at her best, thought Miss Tonks, although Lord Eston, who had changed into evening dress, seemed now quite intimidating, made remote by elegant tailoring.

"I called on you the day after the ball," said Lord Eston to Cassandra. "I was told you were resting in your room."

"I wasn't," replied Cassandra. "I left during the night with Aunt Letitia."

"Why?"

"Because . . . because of my rudeness to you, I was to be sent to a seminary in Bath. Aunt Letitia had been ordered from the house. I thought the best solution would be to accompany Aunt to London."

"To the hotel? What work will you do there?"

"Whatever they care to give me."

Miss Tonks sat facing a mirror. She was somewhat comforted by her own reflection. She was wearing a small

45

hat of swathed fabric and curled feathers. Her own brown merino gown was covered with a short plum-coloured spencer with long, close-fitting sleeves. A lady needed such fashionable armour at such a difficult dinner party.

"I am sure there is no need for Cassandra to *work*," she said quickly. "My sister will soon come to her senses."

"I do not intend to be a parasite," pointed out Cassandra.

Dinner was well cooked. Fish in oyster sauce was followed by boiled beef and vegetables, neck of pork roasted with apple sauce, hashed turkey, mutton steaks, salad, roasted wild duck, fried rabbits, and then a plum pudding and tartlets. To Miss Tonks's dismay, Cassandra ate with a hearty appetite. She herself had perfected the art of appearing to take little while managing to consume quite a lot and thought Honoria must be even more lacking in the social graces than she had previously imagined, for Cassandra had been badly instructed.

Lord Eston amused them during dinner with gossip and tittle-tattle about this and that. Miss Tonks did her best to supply some amusing anecdotes of her own, or rather of Lady Fortescue's own, while darting anxious little glances at her niece, who was not making any effort to please.

But towards the end of the meal, Miss Tonks realized she would need to excuse herself and make use of the chamberpot under the bed in the room she shared with Cassandra. She arose and murmured something and left the couple alone.

"I admire your spirit of rebellion, Miss Cassandra," said Lord Eston. "But what will happen to you in the future? As I recall from gossip, these owners of the Poor Relation are even more antique than your aunt. What will you do when they shuffle off this mortal coil?"

"Perhaps by that time," said Cassandra, "I shall be considered old enough to make a suitable governess."

"Now that is a sorry life. Few governesses manage to find a comfortable establishment. They are treated with contempt by the servants and masters alike. Often the unwanted attentions of the master or the grown sons of the house are thrust upon her."

Cassandra smiled. "As to that, I am quite plain, my lord, and therefore not likely to receive any over-warm attentions."

"You are not plain to my eyes, freckle face. But even were you an absolute Friday-faced antidote, then that would not protect you. Men in their cups will attack anything vulnerable. I would see you better protected."

"There must be a way for a female to survive in this world without the aid of men," said Cassandra. "Perhaps the Blue Stockings of London will adopt me."

"Then I hope your education has been of a high order. Despite popular opinion, any Blue Stocking with enough charity to take you under her wing would expect you to have a singularly well educated and informed mind."

Cassandra coloured. "I fear my education is only that considered sufficient for a female. I sew and paint and sing badly. I really should go and see what is keeping Miss Tonks."

"No, stay. She will be with us soon enough. Some more wine?"

"If you please. I do not normally drink anything much stronger than lemonade and I hope I do not become foxed."

"I will let you know if there is any danger of that happening. So let us return to your prospects. You have obviously put all thoughts of marriage behind you."

"Why?"

"Unless your parents are forgiving enough to supply you with a large dowry, then it will take a very strong gentleman indeed who would want to marry a glorified servant."

"You are rude."

"As you are. That snub at the ball was quite a facer. I cried all night. But let us be practical. You are not made to be a spinster."

"Spoken like a very man! May I remind you, my lord, that spinsters usually do not choose their lot in life. It is chosen for them. Lack of looks or, more often, lack of money."

"But you have chosen such a fate by your actions."

"What would you? Should I have meekly stood by and let them send me to that house of correction called a seminary in Bath? Should I have let Aunt Letitia walk unaccompanied in the middle of the night to the nearest inn?"

"I admire your spirit. But I am sure your parents will travel to London as soon as possible to reclaim you, and by that time, you might be glad to go with them."

"I am tired of talking about me," said Cassandra, wondering what on earth was keeping Miss Tonks. "I am sorry I was so rude to you at the ball, but the way I was being thrust upon you was the outside of enough. What of you? Do you plan to find a bride?"

"I think I might." He looked thoughtfully at her and his gaze fell to her soft and generous mouth. Cassandra hurriedly drank more wine to cover her sudden confusion. The air was suddenly full of sexual tension, although she did not know that, only being aware of a suffocated nervous feeling and a virginal awareness of danger. But when she looked up again into his lazy blue eyes, they showed nothing but interested amusement. "Will you find someone for me, Miss Cassandra, to save me the trouble of courting? I am not the poem-writing, languishing type."

"Then you have never been in love," said Cassandra,

suddenly thinking of the highwayman. "Anyone in love finds it quite easy to be ridiculous."

"Love? What do you know of love?"

"Enough," said Cassandra, tilting up her small stubborn chin.

He sighed. "A lot of nonsense is talked about love and romance. Falling in love is an ephemeral thing, and the emotions engendered thereby do not last. If one is lucky, it is followed by all the difficulties of real love, or so I have observed."

"How cynical," said Cassandra, but thinking all the while that if she really fell in love with, say, her highwayman, such a love would last a lifetime.

"I have a good friend, Toby Humphrey. He fell in love with a certain Miss Darwin. Miss Darwin was admittedly an enchanting, dainty creature, like a fairy. She had little fortune and a tiresome family. But Toby was determined to marry her, and he did. A year of enchantment set in for Toby. He walked on air. But at the end of that year, the tide of passion receded and facing him across the breakfast table was an empty-headed little creature. Her baby talk, her lisp, which so recently drove him to ecstasies, grated day by day on his nerves. He became worried about the money she was spending on new gowns, money which he had gladly paid out to adorn his beloved at the height of his infatuation."

"And so what did he do?"

"He rejoined the army, and from the safe distance of the Iberian Peninsula he writes her passionate love letters, not meaning a word of them, but grateful to her for not having stood in the way of his freedom."

"Poor lady."

"Oh, no, she is extremely happy. She has a pretty little villa at Norwood, she has these beautiful letters from her brave and devoted husband to read to her admiring friends;

and said husband, who had become a tiresome bear, is around no longer to plague her."

"This is a ridiculous conversation. Very few people in society marry for love and you know it."

"And very sensible too. Less people around to suffer the miseries of disappointment."

Cassandra rested her chin on her hands and surveyed him. "So you will choose a lady with a good pedigree and a good dowry, and after she has produced an heir for you, you will forget about her."

For some reason, Lord Eston felt his good humour fading fast. In fact, this was exactly what he had had in mind before he had come across this gauche hoyden with her freckled face and blunt manners.

Sensing his anger, Cassandra said, "I look forward to my new role in life. I shall not be expected to dress like a fashion plate. You men are lucky. You do not suffer the tyrannies of fashion."

He raised his hands in mock horror. "I am a slave to my tailor. What vile language his breed have for colours. 'What think you, my lord,' he says, 'of the Emperor's Eye, the Mud of Paris, the Sigh Supprest?' He even orders me to have pantaloons of a reddish colour. 'All on the reds now, my lord.' It is even regulated whether the coat shall be worn open or buttoned, and if buttoned, whether by one button or two, and by which. Sometimes a cane is to be carried in the hand, sometimes a club, sometimes a common twig. Just recently it was the vogue for every man to walk the streets with his hands thrust into his coat pockets. The length of the neck handkerchief, the shape, the mode of tying it, must all be in the mode. There is a professor in Bond Street, who, in lessons, at half a guinea, instructs gentlemen in the art of tying their neck handkerchiefs in the newest and most approved style."

The door opened and Miss Tonks crept apologetically

in. Her nose was red with cold and the hem of her gown was wet. Cassandra wondered if Miss Tonks had been foolish enough to venture to the outside privy in a snow-storm.

But Miss Tonks had made use of the chamber-pot in her room but had then gone into an agony of debate with herself about what to do with the contents. Slops were expected to be left until the morning, when a servant carried them away. But it went against her fastidious soul to have such a thing in the bedchamber. She had opened the window to throw the contents out but had been driven back by the fury of the storm. She was too shy to summon a servant to perform the task for her and so, covering the chamber-pot with a linen cloth, she had crept downstairs and out into the howling whiteness of the inn yard and deposited the contents in a corner.

"You are surely not drinking port on top of the wine we had for dinner, Cassandra," she exclaimed. "Do, my lord, call for some soda water. I know gentlemen are accustomed to the Horrors"—the Horrors being the polite name for delirium tremens—"but it is not a suitable thing to happen to a lady."

Lord Eston sent for soda water and then suggested a game of cribbage. Cassandra, who was beginning to find his presence oppressive, opened her mouth to refuse but was forestalled by Miss Tonks, who quickly agreed. They played for pennies. Outside the inn, the world fell silent, enclosed and muffled in deep snow.

At nine o'clock, Lord Eston suggested they retire for the night, twitching back the curtain as he spoke. In the light of the posting-house lamp swinging over the arched entrance he could see snow blowing in the wind.

"We may as well settle down for a long siege," he said. "I do not know when we will be able to travel again."

Miss Tonks bit back a moan. The diamonds in the foot

of her trunk seemed to flash and burn in her guilty mind.

Cassandra stood up and curtsied to Lord Eston and then hesitated in the doorway. "Is this a *very* expensive posting-house, my lord?"

"I am afraid so. I will take care of your bills. And," he added quickly, noticing the mulish tilt of that chin, "you may pay me when you can."

"I will pay you out of my wages," said Cassandra proudly.

"Oh, dear," twittered Miss Tonks, "we do not actually take wages. But, my dear Lord Eston, I myself will settle the account out of my share of the profits." A slow smile dawned on her thin face. "Goodness, I suddenly feel like a woman of business at last. Quite like Rothschild! Come, Cassandra."

The bad weather, not so dramatic in London as in the country, was nonetheless miserable enough to exacerbate tempers at the Poor Relation. Funds were running very low indeed and Despard, the cook, was performing miracles of cuisine with the most inexpensive ingredients, although such economies offended him greatly, prompting Sir Philip to say waspishly that there was no one more extravagant than a radical, "always so good at spending *other* people's money."

Two of the unpaid waiters left for the new hotel, Tupple's, which meant that Lady Fortescue and Colonel Sandhurst really had to wait table in the dining-room instead of just playing at it. Then two chambermaids left, and it fell to Mrs. Budley to turn her hand to cleaning and making beds. The fact that Sir Philip appeared to consider all work beneath him roused the ire of the others. All were working except him. Betty and John, Lady Fortescue's old servants, who had hitherto had the luxury of only waiting on the poor relations, had to be delegated to the kitchen when two of Despard's staff walked out. Tempers rose when Sir Philip informed them that he had called in at Tupple's and found the late staff all appeared to be working there.

"It is my belief they are luring them away in order to break us," said Lady Fortescue. "Oh, for some money. Our credit is stretched to the limit."

"The day has been warmer," said the colonel, "and the snow is beginning to melt. Perhaps Miss Tonks will be with us soon."

"Miss Tonks!" jeered Sir Philip. "She will eventually arrive back, twittering and apologizing and saying she just could not *dare* take anything."

"Matters might be helped if you did some work," snapped the colonel. "Lady Fortescue is feeling exhausted with all the running up and down stairs."

"Lady Fortescue never runs," pointed out Sir Philip. "She moves as stately as a flagship on a calm sea." He leered roguishly at Lady Fortescue, who, to the colonel's fury, smiled indulgently at the old horror.

"I have been thinking," said the colonel, "that perhaps if we sold this place, Lady Fortescue and I could retire to somewhere in the country."

"What?" demanded Sir Philip wrathfully. "This is her house to sell, not yours. Why should she want to bury herself in the country with an old stick like you anyway?"

"I have discussed the matter with Colonel Sandhurst," said Lady Fortescue. "Things are going from bad to worse. I am so very tired."

"I'll work in the dining-room for you, dear lady," said Sir Philip. "You have a few days' rest. Leave it all to me."

"Thank you." Lady Fortescue leaned back in her chair and closed her eyes.

The colonel glared at Sir Philip. He himself had been working alongside Lady Fortescue, and yet she had thanked this old fright for volunteering to do what he should have been doing for days.

If only Miss Tonks . . . But Miss Tonks! The colonel shook his head sadly. They should never have relied on her.

Chapter Four

The ruling passion, be it what it will,
The ruling passion conquers reason still.
—ALEXANDER POPE

MISS TONKS and Cassandra, travelling in yet another post-chaise, arrived on the outskirts of London two weeks after having been snow-bound at the posting-house.

Miss Tonks's rosy dreams of her triumphal arrival home were somewhat marred by a nagging worry. The day following their dinner with Lord Eston had been spent pleasantly in conversation and cards. Lord Eston and Cassandra appeared to be easy in each other's company. Miss Tonks, despite her earlier misgivings about Lord Eston, began to hope that romance might blossom between the pair, that she might be able to achieve for Cassandra what her mother could not. But just before dinner, an elderly gentleman by the name of Sir Andrew Boyle had called. It transpired Sir Andrew was an old friend of Lord Eston's family and lived at the manor-house near the posting-house. His servants, he said, had just cleared the drive and the snow had stopped falling. He urged Lord Eston to stay at the manor until the roads were clear enough for him to proceed on his journey. Sir Andrew added that his granddaughter, Amanda, grew more beautiful every day and would be delighted to see him. And to Miss Tonks's surprise, Lord Eston had left, just like that.

She was puzzled. He had not even introduced them to Sir Andrew. He had arranged that all their bills at the posting-house were to be forwarded to him. He did not say anything to Cassandra about wishing to see her again.

Miss Tonks hung her head. It was all because they were both now in trade, she thought sadly. Obviously they were only good enough to amuse Lord Eston when he had no prospect of more fashionable company. Still, it was very lowering during their long stay at the posting-house to know that he was hard by at the manor and did not even trouble to call. She had finally kept her thoughts and speculations to herself because Cassandra would only laugh and say that obviously the charms of this Amanda were keeping him well occupied. Miss Tonks could not help remembering surprising an expression of warmth and affection on his face as Lord Eston had looked at Cassandra when she had had her head bent over the game of cribbage. He had not seemed at all high in the instep either, treating her, Miss Tonks, like an equal, paying their bills at the posting-house, not to mention having stolen the diamonds for her. So why had he left? Why, why, why?

But soon they would be home, or what passed for home these days. She must not let Cassandra be there when she told the others about her great theft. Miss Tonks rubbed the glass of the post-chaise with her glove and looked out into the failing light. The amount of travellers on the Great Western Road never failed to amaze her: horsemen and footmen, carriages of every description and every shape, wagons and carts and covered carts, stage-coaches, long, square, and double coaches, chariots, chaises, gigs, buggies, curricles and phaetons. The sound of wheels ploughing through the wet gravel of the road was as constant and incessant as the roar of the waves on a pebble beach. Then suddenly the sharp thundery rumble of the post-chaise as the wheels left the gravel to lurch over the cobblestones of Hyde Park Corner. Just a little way to go now.

And here was Bond Street at last. Here was the hotel. "I will take you to your room next door first," said Miss Tonks. "While you change, I shall warn the others of your arrival."

"But you must rest first," said Cassandra. "It has been a long and tiring journey."

"No, no, my dear. See, we are arrived." Miss Tonks efficiently paid off the post-chaise and tipped the driver. A servant came out of the hotel to carry in their luggage. "Take my trunk into the hotel," said Miss Tonks, "but take Miss Cassandra's belongings to the apartment next door and show her to the little room next to mine. No, don't fuss, my dear. I shall be with you directly. Just follow Bill here and he will show you where to go."

Bill, the servant, placed Miss Tonks's trunk in the entrance hall under the glittering chandelier which Sir Philip had managed to obtain from a relative and then went off with Cassandra. Miss Tonks took a deep breath and looked around. See, the conquering heroine comes!

Mrs. Budley came tripping down the stairs. "Oh, you are back, Letitia!" she cried, the two ladies having reached that intimate stage of friendship of calling each other by their first names. "How glad I am to see you! Such troubles. Tupple's Hotel is luring our servants away, which is easy for them to do, for we have not paid them. But you must not worry about that. We should never have sent you on such a dangerous expedition."

Miss Tonks espied the hotel porter, who was slouching in the corner with the half-insolent, half-defiant look of the unpaid servant. "Carry my trunk up to our sitting-room," ordered Miss Tonks. "Are the others up there, Eliza?"

"Yes, just sitting down to the tea-tray. What vile weather it has been."

They walked up to the little sitting-room at the top of the house. "Put my trunk there . . . right in the middle of the floor," ordered Miss Tonks.

She waited until the porter had left, opening the door and peering round it to make sure he had actually gone.

"My stars and garters," said Sir Philip, "from all this caution it appears to me that Miss Tonks has really taken something. What is it, Miss Tonks? Your own silver christening spoon?"

"We are happy to have you back safe and well," remarked the colonel with a hard look at Sir Philip. "Anything else is of little consequence."

"Yes, indeed," said Lady Fortescue. "We have been having such a tiresome time of it, Miss Tonks, but no doubt we shall pull through."

"Wait!" Miss Tonks beamed proudly round the small room. *"Voilà!"* She threw back the lid of her trunk.

"What's Viola got to do with it?" grumbled Sir Philip.

"She's telling us to look, you nincompoop," said Lady Fortescue.

"What at? All I can see are a lot of . . ."

Sir Philip's voice tailed away in amazement. For Miss Tonks had seized the tiara and necklace and was holding both of them up. Diamonds flashed and blazed, casting prisms of light on the circle of astonished faces.

Lady Fortescue groped for the colonel's hand and, having found it, held it tightly.

"How did you do it?" she asked. "Won't your sister be after you with the Runners?"

Here was Miss Tonks's big moment, although she felt a qualm at the lie she was about to tell. But fired by the veiled look of jealousy on Sir Philip's face, she said boldly, "I dressed as a *highwayman* and held up my sister's coach!"

"You are a veritable Amazon," said the colonel. "Begin at the beginning and tell us the whole story."

They listened eagerly until Miss Tonks reached the bit about bringing Cassandra with her. "This will not do," said Lady Fortescue severely. "The girl sounds like a hoyden and you should not have encouraged her in this folly. You must take her back immediately." Her face softened. "Do not look so distressed. One of us will take her back. You are a brave lady and have done more than enough. But you must surely see that the girl will ruin all her chances of marriage if she stays with us."

"Harriet James was our *cook* and *she* married the Duke of Rowcester," said Mrs. Budley, leaping to her friend's defence.

"That was a different matter. My nephew had been enamored of Miss James for some years. Where is Miss Cassandra now?"

"I placed her in the small room next to mine," said Miss Tonks. "And she is not a hoyden. She is a dear girl. A trifle blunt but . . ."

"Lady Fortescue has the right of it," said the colonel heavily. "I myself will accompany this young lady to her home. Miss Tonks, you said you had stayed about two weeks at a posting-house. Did Miss Cassandra pay the shot?"

"No, Lord Eston did that. Cassandra did have money, but only enough for a couple of nights. It was such a dreadfully expensive place. His lordship is such a charming gentleman. He is a neighbour of my sister, and Honoria had high hopes of making a match of it between this Lord Eston and Cassandra, which was why all the trouble arose for Cassandra, poor little thing. She, being tired of being humiliated and pushed around, needs must go and insult

Lord Eston at a hunt ball by refusing to dance with him. So Honoria was going to send the child off to one of those dreadful *whipping* seminaries in Bath."

"Quite right, too," said Sir Philip.

"Oh, what have *you* ever got to say that is other than interfering malice?" flashed Miss Tonks. Then her burst of spirit died and she began to weep. "I tried so hard. I thought you would all be so p-pleased."

"We are. We are," said Sir Philip. "Don't cry, for pity's sake. Your nose is turning red."

Miss Tonks threw back her head and faced them all. "Cassandra shall speak for herself," she said. "I am going to fetch her."

There was a silence after she had left, finally broken by Lady Fortescue. "Who would have thought our Miss Tonks would produce such a haul? Goodness, Sir Philip will need to turn these gems into money as soon as possible. Of course it is sad about this wretched girl. She is some spoilt brat who has got to work on Miss Tonks's finer feelings. We'll soon send her to the right-about. You can sell these baubles, can you not, Sir Philip?"

"Easily," he said. "First-class gems. Sell 'em separately."

The colonel got out the account books and he and the others began to discuss what to do with the vast wealth they would get for the diamonds. Sir Philip, while they talked, picked up the tiara and turned it round in his hands, admiring the sparkle. Then he raised it and put it on top of his head.

The door opened and Miss Tonks and Cassandra walked in. Not much out of the common way, thought Lady Fortescue when she saw Cassandra.

But Cassandra looked at Sir Philip, who had risen to his feet and was staring at her, the diamond tiara a little askew on his head, and her face lit up and her eyes sparkled with amusement, causing Lady Fortescue to reverse her first judgement.

Miss Tonks, after winking desperately and grimacing at Sir Philip to try to get him to hide the diamonds, introduced Cassandra all round.

Cassandra sat down on a small sofa next to Mrs. Budley. "Pray be seated, gentlemen," she said to the colonel and Sir Philip. "Now, I gather you have decided that I am to be sent home. It will not answer. Having come all this way, I have no intention of returning to Mama to be sent on to a seminary in Bath. I am old enough to make my own decisions. I am young and strong and willing to work. Do not give me a jaw-me-dead about ruining my chances of marriage. I am no longer interested in marriage. I have already had one Season where I did not take. You should not frown at the idea of another social outcast in your ranks, particularly a young one. If you persist in having nothing to do with me, you leave me no alternative but to seek employ elsewhere." She looked at the tiara, which Sir Philip was placing on the trunk next to the diamond necklace and exclaimed, "Why! That is exactly like Mama's gems which the highwayman stole." The poor relations looked at each other in alarm. They had assumed Miss Tonks had told her niece how she had come by the jewels.

"Oh, those," said Mrs. Budley, picking them up. "Amazing how *ordinary* diamonds are. Have you not noticed how one diamond tiara and one necklace looks like any other? These are the last of my valuables, Miss Cassandra. Sir Philip is going to sell the gems to raise money we sorely need for the hotel."

Cassandra promptly dismissed the jewels from her mind and her large eyes began to sparkle with mischief. "I have just had a great idea. I hear that Tupple's Hotel has been poaching your servants. So why not give me a little money and I will take up residence in Tupple's Hotel for a week, say, and do my best to ruin their reputation."

"How can a young miss stay alone at a London hotel, however fashionable?" exclaimed the colonel.

"Miss Tonks could go with me as my companion," said Cassandra eagerly. "See! I can be of use to you. No one knows me in London."

"But some of the staff of Tupple's might recognize Miss Tonks," Lady Fortescue pointed out.

"I doubt that," said Sir Philip slowly. "She don't work downstairs when she does do any work. And we can disguise her. Might be something in this plan. I'll tell you why. We know that this hotel was deliberately set on fire and Harriet damn' near killed."

"Ladies present," growled the colonel.

"Oh, very well. 'Pologies. Very nearly killed. The more I think of it, the more I think Tupple's was behind it. All the other hotels are mostly for gentlemen. Ours, until they came on the scene, was the only aristocratic family hotel. It would be interesting to know who runs it . . ."

"Anyone knows that," snapped the colonel. "Frenchman by the name of Bonnard."

"Yes, but what kind of Frenchie, hey? Crook? Get Miss Cassandra to spy out the land."

"If Tupple's—however they came by that name—was behind the fire, then you would be sending two gentle ladies into danger."

"Miss Tonks has proved herself a Trojan," said Sir Philip, and Miss Tonks blushed with pleasure. "And Miss Cassandra don't look much good to me for the ballroom or rout but she's got brains in her cockloft. I say, send her. Anyway, while you are all arguifying, I'll take these pretty trinkets and come back with some of the readies."

Sir Philip picked up the gems and scuttled off with his odd crabwise walk.

"I beg you to forget this mad idea," said Colonel Sandhurst.

"Stay a bit." Lady Fortescue put a mittened hand on the colonel's sleeve. Her black eyes rested steadily on Cassandra. "You have bottom, my dear. I do not see how you could come to any harm."

"I think now that Letitia could do anything," said Mrs. Budley, her large pansy eyes filled with admiration.

Miss Tonks flashed her a warning look. Cassandra must never know about the identity of that highwayman, nor that her aunt had been instrumental in Lord Eston's robbing her mother. It was just as well that Honoria's diamonds had not been antique heirlooms but new and set in a pattern quite common in a rich society which often went to balls and parties so overloaded with jewels that one lady brought her footman to follow her around with a chair so that she might frequently rest, so great was the weight of the gems adorning her.

"We will discuss this further when Sir Philip returns. There is one thing that makes me curious," said Lady Fortescue. "This Lord Eston who is a neighbour of yours, Miss Cassandra. I gather your disgrace was because you cut him at some ball, and yet this lord paid your shot at a posting-house. Could it be that he is interested in you? Has formed a tendre for you?"

"I amuse him," began Cassandra, but the colonel interrupted with an exclamation. "Eston. That's it. Thought that name was familiar. In the *Post* this morning. Got engaged to some female. I have it. Amanda Boyle."

So that was why he had never called, thought Miss Tonks dismally. And yet he had seemed to like Cassandra. This was surely evidence then of how badly Cassandra had ruined any hopes of marriage. How did Cassandra feel about the engagement?

But the news seemed to have had no effect on Cassandra at all. She immediately began to make plans. "I cannot stay at Tupple's under my own name," she said. "I know, I shall be some minor foreign royalty travelling incognito. And Aunt Letitia shall be my companion. Hungarian, I think. Most of the people in England do not even know where Hungary is."

"Your accent would give you away," the colonel pointed out.

"Not necessarily," said Lady Fortescue. "A number of high-bred foreigners speak English very well, for they employ English governesses. Miss Cassandra, it is indeed a good idea. But when you have found out what we require, I beg of you to return home. Your mother by that time will have come to her senses. No, do not grin in that boyish way. Not suitable in any female, either foreign or otherwise. Decorum at all times, and never betray an excess of emotion. It offends, and besides, causes wrinkles."

"We will see," said Cassandra demurely, but with a subdued air of triumph. This was the life for her, a life like that of her darling highwayman, a life of adventure.

Lady Fortescue reflected, as they began to discuss plans for Cassandra's impersonation, that there was something very engaging and likeable about the girl. Such a pity about Lord Eston. Good family, rich by all accounts, and eminently suitable. Who were the Boyles anyway? She racked her long memory. She could remember a Sir Andrew Boyle who had once courted her. Gentry, not aristocracy. Her family had frowned on his attentions and so he had married a . . . Lady Fortescue's memory failed her at this point.

Lady Fortescue had quickly gathered that Cassandra had no idea who the highwayman was who held up her mother's coach. "Were you with your mother when the highwayman took the diamonds from her?" she asked.

"Yes, we were on our way to a ball."

"How frightful," exclaimed Mrs. Budley. "But of course he would not be interested in you because all he wanted was your mother's jewels," Mrs. Budley said, thinking the highwayman had been Letitia Tonks.

Cassandra turned a trifle pink but her eyes sparkled. "As a matter of fact, the wicked rogue did steal something from me."

"What was that, my dear?" asked the colonel, giving a sideways look of reproach at Miss Tonks.

"He stole a kiss."

There was a shocked silence. Everyone except Cassandra looked hard at Miss Tonks, who looked at the floor.

"How nasty for you," said Lady Fortescue faintly. "Such things are best forgotten."

"Oh, no, he was very dashing and I rather enjoyed it," said Cassandra blithely.

Again that shocked silence. Mrs. Budley twisted her handkerchief uneasily in her hands. She had heard there were women who preferred their own sex. And she herself shared a bed with Letitia!

"Why so solemn!" exclaimed Cassandra at last. "Let us forget about highwaymen and get down to business!"

Lord Eston had forgotten all his lectures on love to Miss Cassandra Blessop. He was enchanted with Amanda Boyle and had been from the minute he set eyes on her. He even forgot that the reason he had accepted Sir Andrew's invitation with alacrity was because he had felt himself in danger of falling in love with Cassandra, and much as he still thought her a splendid sort of girl, he had come to the conclusion that she lacked the necessary characteristics for a good wife. She was too independently minded, too forthright, too blunt—admirable qualities in a man but hardly the stuff that dreams were made of.

But Amanda, on the other hand, ah, there was perfection—from the topknot of her glossy brown hair to her tiny feet. She was a dainty little thing with huge blue eyes like the summer sea, a tiny straight nose, and a perfect little mouth. She was all frills and lace. She sang like an angel. The first evening at the manor when he had been debating whether he should return to the posting-house and apologize for his abrupt departure, she had started to sing, accompanying herself on the harp. From that moment he was lost. He regretted the battles he had fought and the mistresses he had kept. He felt he should have come to her virginal and unsullied. The fact that her father and mother were a rather grasping pair and that her brood of brothers and sisters were spoilt to a fault did not alter his desire to make her his bride.

When he asked for her hand in marriage, Mr. Boyle had given his permission on the spot. Lord Eston had been allowed to kiss Amanda. Of course that kiss had none of the heady sweetness that he remembered experiencing when Cassandra's mouth had been under his own, but he felt an almost spiritual happiness.

His thoughts, however, returned to Cassandra again when Mr. and Mrs. Boyle said they had a long-standing engagement to travel to London to visit Mrs. Boyle's sister, and for that reason had booked a suite of rooms at the new hotel, Tupple's.

Lord Eston offered them his town house but was told it would not answer until he and Amanda were married. He was surprised that the Boyles were not to stay with Mrs. Boyle's sister, Mrs. Tabitha Sinclair in Green Street, but Mrs. Boyle said her dear sister was in too poor health to entertain them. The facts, which were not told to Lord Eston, were that Mrs. Sinclair was believed to be on the point of death and Mrs. Boyle wanted to make sure that either she herself or her children should inherit. Mrs. Sinclair detested her sister and brother-in-law, but now that she was dying, Mrs. Boyle had high hopes of a deathbed reconciliation leading to a profitable will. Lord Eston suggested they stay at the Poor Relation but Mrs. Boyle said it was owned by eccentrics and Tupple's would do very well. He offered them his escort to London, and although he pressed Mr. Boyle to get Amanda to agree to an early wedding by special licence, Mr. Boyle replied that it would be a shameful thing to do his daughter out of a grand wedding with all her friends and relatives present, and that, anyway, a rushed wedding gave society fuel for gossip, which was all pretty much what Amanda had said herself, except in such a delicate and halting way that it made Lord Eston feel like a slavering satyr. He should be able to curb his lusts, he thought ruefully, for a few more months.

It was an exhausting journey to London although the roads were clear, because not only was Amanda sick with the motion of the coach but her pet pug was sick, too. He could only be grateful that her brothers and sisters had been left with a cousin in the country. Looking after Amanda was enough. But in fact Lord Eston saw little of his beloved except to help carry her to and from various postinghouses, marvelling at the fragility of the beautiful body he held in his arms and wondering what it would be like to eventually possess it.

It was when he deposited the Boyle family at Tupple's that his thoughts turned once more to Cassandra and Miss Tonks. Mrs. Boyle told him in a hushed voice that poor little Amanda was too fatigued by the journey to entertain him that evening. He went to his town house, changed into his evening clothes and decided to call at the Poor Relation Hotel and pay his respects to Miss Tonks—and Cassandra, of course.

Sir Philip was squatting on a high stool behind the reception desk when he walked into the entrance hall. Lord Eston looked around curiously. There was no doubt that this hotel had a certain air that Tupple's lacked. The crystal chandelier was magnificent. The gnomish man in the ghastly brown wig behind the reception was another matter. Lord Eston approached Sir Philip.

"I am come to pay my respects to Miss Cassandra Blessop and Miss Tonks."

Sir Philip smiled horribly, revealing a set of china false teeth, while all the time his busy brain was wondering whether Miss Tonks had confided in this Lord Eston and decided she probably had. On the other hand, he could hardly tell Lord Eston that Miss Tonks and her niece were masquerading as Hungarian royalty.

"I am afraid they are gone to the country," said Sir Philip.

Lord Eston was startled. Cassandra was surely the sort of young lady who would stick to her guns. On the other hand, these weird people who ran this hotel might have turned her away.

He felt disappointed and at the same time irritated with himself. He should really have called on them at the posting-house. The more he thought of it, the more bad-mannered his behavior seemed to him, particularly as Cassandra was no longer in his mind a danger, but merely a spirited girl he had once met.

"Thank you," he said rather bleakly and turned and left.

He made his way to his club, White's in St. James's. He saw, on entering the coffee room, Peter Blaney, an old army friend, and hailed him with delight. "When did you return?" asked Lord Eston.

"Got invalided home," said Mr. Blaney with his shy smile. He was thirty and war-hardened but looked twenty and incredibly naïve and innocent, attributes he put to profitable use at the card-table. "What's this I hear? You are to wed the Boyle girl?"

"I am the luckiest of men."

"I never met the daughter," said Mr. Blaney, "but I know the parents. Have they asked you for money yet?"

"No."

"They will, my dear fellow. They will."

A faint look of hauteur came into Lord Eston's handsome face. "I think you must be thinking of another family."

"Probably. Not an uncommon name. I was thinking of the Oxfordshire Boyles at Hayley Manor."

"And in what way do these Boyles you were speaking of ask you for money?" demanded Lord Eston, who had no intention of admitting that the Boyles his friend was talking about and his future in-laws were one and the same. "I assume they asked *you*. I mean, not like you to pass along gossip."

"Oh, it was indeed I. The first time was when I was on leave two years ago and they were up for the Season with some moppet of a little girl, although she was too young to be out." He looked embarrassed. "I am sorry. I seem to be putting my foot in it all round. Possibly that moppet is now to be your future bride, although, come to think of it, we are talking about the Oxfordshire Boyles." He looked curiously at his friend but Lord Eston's face remained a well-bred blank. "Anyway, about the money. He said he had discovered an inventor who had plans for a mechanical corn-thresher operated by steam which would save heaps of money on employing workers. All this chap needed was the money to buy the materials to perfect this design."

"How much?"

"Two thousand guineas?"

"*That* much?"

"I asked if said machinery was to be gold-plated but he said that should I put up the readies, the machine would be made and presented to my father, who is keen on all the latest innovations in agriculture, along with the patent. Now my old man's birthday was coming up and it did seem like quite a splendid present, but I asked Boyle what *he* got out of it, and he said piously that he merely wanted to help genius along. Well, I had some prize money and was prepared to pay up. But caution prompted me to offer him a bill of exchange."

Lord Eston nodded his understanding. Even at this early part of the nineteenth century the main instrument of the London money market was the bill of exchange, which was the written acknowledgement of the existence of a debt, an I.O.U. recording the debtor's undertaking to pay at a specified date.

"I asked whom it was to be made out to and he said to make it out to him, Henry Boyle. I said, 'Why not this inventor?' 'I handle all his money matters,' he said airily. I don't know why, but I became suspicious and said I had changed my mind. I did not have the money available. A year later, I met Chuffy Byng, who was spitting with fury. Seems he had paid Boyle for said invention, Boyle had taken the money and given him in return a piece of paper offering to hand over the patent of the invention at such time as the machine would be completed and patented. Every time Chuffy asked about it, he was told the inventor had not yet completed his work, and to add insult to injury, Boyle tried to get *more* money out of Chuffy to complete the invention."

"Anything else?" asked Lord Eston, thinking there was no hope there could be two Henry Boyles living at Hayley Manor in Oxfordshire.

"There's worse. Goodness, I'm glad they're obviously not your Boyles. Chuffy decided to take Boyle to court and sent a note round to say he would be calling on him. The Boyles were living with some relative in Green Street at that time.

"When he arrived, he was told that Boyle was from home but that Mrs. Boyle would receive him. He thought he may as well have a word with her and find out when old man Boyle was due to return. She served him tea and as he was raising his cup to his lips, Mrs. Boyle ups and screams, 'Rape! Rape!' and tears open the front of her gown and falls on the floor as the servants rush in. Chaos all round. Burnt feathers, sal volatile, accusations, recriminations, monster and beast, and there suddenly is Boyle himself, crying out about the assault on his wife. Well, when the dust settled, the sweating Chuffy was more or less told if he forgot about the invention and courts and suchlike, nothing would be said about his trying to rape Mrs. B. He was so grateful to get shot of the lot of them that he dropped the whole matter."

Lord Eston said slowly, "I wasn't going to tell you, but my future in-laws are the Boyles of Hayley Manor."

"I am sorry. Shouldn't have opened my mouth."

"I would be grateful if you didn't open it to anyone else about this matter. My poor Amanda is such an innocent, she will know nothing of her parents' machinations. Once we are married, I will make sure she sees as little as possible of them."

"Let's have a bottle of the best burgundy and drink your health," said Mr. Blaney, "and talk of other things. Did you hear about Jerry Anderson?"

"What about him?"

"He bought Nancy Girl from Lord Cusp."

"That nasty-tempered mare! Fine-looking beast but a bad disposition and a worse pedigree. You can pretty much tell an animal from its pedigree. Bad forebears make bad horses."

71

"And people, too," remarked Mr. Blaney cheerfully and then, looking at Lord Eston's stiff face, regretted his words.

Lady Fortescue and the colonel were waiting until Sir Philip returned to their hotel sitting-room. He had gone to sell more of the diamonds which he had prized loose from their moorings.

"Plenty of money," he chortled as he entered, "and I only sold the necklace. Keep the tiara in reserve. Told the servants we'd pay them tomorrow and increase their wages. We'll only increase them by a fraction, but that news will travel to those traitors who went to Tupple's. They'll be replaced tomorrow. Lots of lovely money to keep us in funds for a long time. Hey, ho, who would have thought our Miss Tonks had so much bottom?"

"She is a surprising lady," said Lady Fortescue stiffly while the colonel glowered.

"What's this? What's happened?" Sir Philip peered at them. "She was the heroine of the year before she left to go to Tupple's."

"We did not tell you before, but we learned from Miss Cassandra," said Lady Fortescue, one hand resting on the silver knob of her ebony cane, "that this highwayman, who we know to have been Miss Tonks although Miss Cassandra does not, kissed her."

"Wait a bit!" Sir Philip goggled. "Do you mean Letitia Tonks bussed her own niece?"

"That is exactly what I mean."

Sir Philip kicked up his little legs and roared with laughter. Then he jumped to his feet and paraded around the room, quoting Lord Byron.

"The isles of Greece, the isles of Greece!
Where burning Sappho loved and sung . . ."

Then he stopped and swung round. "Where is our Sappho now?"

"At Tupple's as companion to Cassandra."

"But hitherto she's been sharing a bed with Mrs. Budley?" Sir Philip rubbed his dry old hands together. "My, my! This is wonderful! Poor Mrs. Budley."

"Silence!" roared the colonel. "We are sure that Miss Tonks was simply acting out her part of highwayman. In romances, the highwayman always kisses the heroine."

Sir Philip sniggered. "Not a very charming experience for our Miss Cassandra."

"Fortunately," said Lady Fortescue, "she said she liked it."

"Two of them! Odd's Fish, no wonder the child is not interested in marriage."

"I am convinced it is a case of innocence on both sides," snapped Lady Fortescue. "And you are to keep your thoughts to yourself, Sir Philip!"

Chapter Five

And, after all, what is a lie? 'Tis but
The truth in masquerade.
                          —LORD BYRON

LORD ESTON approached Tupple's Hotel on the following afternoon with a slight feeling of trepidation. He had never scrutinized his future in-laws too closely, and besides, his Amanda had cast a rosy glow around everyone near her. He felt sure when he saw her again that all his qualms of unease would be dispersed. Amanda was loving and trusting, and if her father was a villain, then she surely knew nothing about it.

The day, however, was in keeping with his mood, slushy and messy, with the crossing-sweepers hard at work.

When he entered the hotel, he was met by the owner, Mr. Bonnard, who bowed low and then proceeded to dance about him as if performing some primitive welcoming rite. "I will inform your fiancée of your arrival, my lord." He kissed the tips of his fingers. "Such grace, such charm!"

Lord Eston looked haughtily down at the sallow-faced little Frenchman. "Keep your remarks to yourself, sirrah," he said, "and announce me."

"But certainly, certainly. If your lordship will have a seat in our new coffee room . . . this way . . . this way. Observe our new tables of the finest mahogany. *Tiens!* There is not a better hotel in the whole of London."

Lord Eston paused on the threshold. There were two ladies in the coffee room, seated by the window. He would have known those freckles anywhere, he thought in surprise, looking hard at the younger one.

"Ah, you hesitate," cried Bonnard from his elbow. He lowered his voice. "Our hotel is honoured. Hungarian royalty. They go under the name of Miss Haldane and her companion, Mrs. Stocks . . . incognito, you see. They have begged me to respect their desire for privacy."

"You are not respecting it by babbling on about it. Leave me."

Bonnard flew off and Lord Eston walked slowly forward. Cassandra was dressed in black and wearing a black lace cap on her red hair. She had obviously tried to age herself by donning sober clothes, but they had the effect of making her look younger than ever. Miss Tonks he only recognized after staring at her very hard. Her cheeks had been puffed out, probably with wax-pads, and she was wearing a blond wig under an enormous turban.

"Good day, ladies," he said.

"Gracious!" Cassandra looked at him wide-eyed. "What are you doing here?"

"I am here to see my fiancée. What is more to the point is, what are you and Miss Tonks doing here, and masquerading as Hungarian royalty?"

"We are spies," said Cassandra cheerfully. "Bonnard has been poaching our servants. We are here to find out what his game is."

"Do not betray us," said Miss Tonks. "But do you not think my disguise very fine? The hotel was set on fire, the

Poor Relation, that is, some time ago, and I feel that Tupple's was behind it."

"I will not betray you." He sat down. He reflected that Miss Tonks was the kind of spinster who probably read too many novels. Burning down the Poor Relation, indeed! "I must apologize for my abrupt departure from the posting-house. I meant to call on you during the following week, but events occurred which put you out of my mind."

"Ah, your engagement," said Cassandra, her large hazel eyes sparkling. "So you have fallen in love at last. I can see it in your face."

He smiled at her happily. "I am the most fortunate of men."

"And you have obviously found a lady of wit and character and humour."

"My Amanda is an angel."

Watching them, Miss Tonks felt quite sour and bitter. Before Cassandra had come with her to London, she had had little opportunity of getting to know her niece. Now she knew her well and loved her. How could Lord Eston be so blind?

"I have forgotten the name of your fiancée's family," said Cassandra.

"Boyle."

Miss Tonks looked at him in surprise. "The Boyles who are resident here?"

"The same."

Cassandra was also looking at him in surprise. "Dear me, I would never have thought . . ."

"Never have thought what, Miss Cassandra?"

"Oh, I thought you were a hardened bachelor." Lord Eston was suddenly sure she had been about to say something else.

Bonnard reappeared. He bowed very low to the ladies

and then said to Lord Eston, "If you will follow me, my lord."

Lord Eston rose and looked down at Cassandra. He was uneasy about her. She was too young to be playing this ridiculous masquerade. She seemed fragile and defenceless with only the odd Miss Tonks to protect her.

"I will call on you later if I may," he said.

"Oh, do that," said Cassandra gaily. "Perhaps we might have another game of cribbage."

Lord Eston followed Bonnard up the stairs. The Boyles had a suite of apartments on the first floor.

Mr. Boyle welcomed him with his usual jovial heartiness and led him into their private sitting-room where Mrs. Boyle and her daughter were seated.

"What's this I hear, Eston?" he cried. "I gather from Bonnard that you are on chatting terms with our Hungarian residents."

"They seem very English to me," commented Lord Eston. "Why do you think they are Hungarian?"

Mr. Boyle put a finger alongside his nose in a vulgar manner. "Bonnard told me. Travelling incognito. Tried to get to know them but frosty, very frosty."

Amanda clasped her little hands. "I would love to meet them. Can you not introduce me?"

Lord Eston sat down beside her on the sofa and smiled at her indulgently. "You really don't want to waste your time with a couple of obscure foreigners, now do you?"

Amanda pouted prettily. "Yes, I would. The younger one, Miss Haldane, she calls herself, has such merry eyes and I am sure we could be the best of friends."

"We'll see," he said evasively. "have you recovered from your journey?"

"I still feel a little unwell, and poor Rupert feels the same." She lifted the little pug up to Lord Eston. "Give poor Rupert a tiny kiss."

"I will save that delight for another time."

Amanda pouted again. "Rupert thinks you don't like him and his ickle heart is breaking."

"There, I'll pat him. Ouch! Does he always bite?"

"Bad Rupert. Jealous Rupert."

There was a scratching at the door and then Bonnard oiled his way into the room. "Mr. Boyle, if I may have a moment of your time?"

What's this all about? wondered Lord Eston. Has Boyle not paid his bill? But then no hotel demands the bill until the stay is over. Why should he be on such familiar terms with this hotelier?

But he saw Amanda gazing at him with that steady blue stare of hers, he saw her shining hair and the delicacy of her features and his heart turned over. Her father could turn out to be Caliban and still he would marry her.

Mrs. Boyle rose and excused herself and, to his delight, Lord Eston found himself alone with Amanda.

He slid an arm around her shoulders and whispered, "One kiss, my dear, before your parents return."

"It's very naughty of you," giggled Amanda. "Oh, my bear is cross. There!"

She puckered up her lips. Her enchanting face seemed to swim before his eyes. He crushed her mouth under his own. She gave a little exclamation against his mouth and then pushed at his shoulders with her hands.

He released her immediately. Her eyes were shining with tears and her lips trembled. "My bear frightens me," she whispered.

He immediately felt remorseful, ugly, and brutal and raised her hand to his lips. "I am sorry," he said softly.

She smiled tremulously and then turned her head away. "I sometimes think you do not love me," she said.

Despite his remorse, he also experienced a surge of

impatience. "My dear, what more can I say? I apologized. I did not mean to be so rough with you."

"It's not that."

"What then? Don't turn your head away."

Her steady blue gaze held his. "If you loved me, you would introduce me to those Hungarian ladies."

"I do not think that very wise. They may not be Hungarian at all. You have only that gossipy creature's, Bonnard's, word for it."

A mulish look settled on her face. She had, he noticed for the first time, a determined chin. "Is this how our marriage is going to be?" she asked petulantly. "Am I to meet no one?"

Mrs. Boyle came into the room just as Lord Eston had begun to say, "Well, I suppose I—"

"Mama," cried Amanda. "Lord Eston is to introduce us to those Hungarian ladies. The chip straw with the blue ribbon, do you think? Or perhaps that is too *summery*. The little velvet one with the gauze trim perhaps? Come with me and help me choose."

Lord Eston had a few moments alone before Mr. Boyle came back. "Sound fellow, that Bonnard," he said, sinking into a chair.

"Are you comfortable here?" Lord Eston looked around. The furniture was not of good quality but painted with a quantity of gilt to give it a spurious air of elegance.

"Oh, yes, food's excellent."

"I believe the Poor Relation has now the best kitchen in London."

"Don't believe what you hear. You need a sound tradesman to run a business. Not an impoverished aristocrat like Lady Fortescue."

"Forgive me for contradicting you, but I have friends who have stayed there and said it was excellent."

"Well, I like to keep an eye on things," said Mr. Boyle

obscurely. He was a thickset man with a high colour. Tufts of hair grew from his nose and ears and he wore a wig low down on his forehead. "Lot of our class," he said, "think they're above trade and that's been the ruin of the aristocracy. I believe you have dealings in the City."

"Stocks and shares, yes."

"Interested in a copper-bottomed venture?"

Here it comes, thought Lord Eston with a sinking heart, the mechanical corn-thresher.

"It depends on the venture," he said cautiously.

"Heard of Jamaica?"

"Yes."

Mr. Boyle leaned forward. "Sugar's the thing," he said eagerly. "Sugar is the new gold. There's a huge plantation for sale and I could get it for us for a rock-bottom price. Old Heatherington's place."

"Sugar plantations employ slave labour," said Lord Eston.

"Yes, and good labour on this one too. None of your imported rubbish but home-grown slaves."

A surprising number of English people detested slavery despite the brutality of the age and Lord Eston was one of them.

But wondering just how far Mr. Boyle was prepared to go, he said, "And what does one do to obtain this plantation?"

"Heatherington don't want to put it on the open market and he trusts me. Says he'd rather sell to a gentleman than some of those Jamaican planters."

"How much?"

Mr. Boyle named a sum that made Lord Eston blink and then went on hurriedly, "Of course, it's not just the land and the house you're paying for but the slaves as well, and good slaves don't come cheap."

"Where is this Mr. Heatherington?"

"He went back."

"But you have plans of the land and details of the yield, have you not?"

"Certainly, certainly. But you young men don't want to bother your heads about business. You just give me a draft on your bank and leave the rest to me."

Lord Eston leaned back in his chair and surveyed his future father-in-law with something approaching admiration. "And when do I get to see this property?"

"What, hey?" Mr. Boyle looked alarmed. "You don't want to *see*." He waved a hand. "Too far away. Rotten voyage. Diseases all over the place."

"But plantations do not run themselves. I would need to appoint a supervisor."

"Got one. Strong man," said Mr. Boyle quickly.

Amanda and her mother came into the room. "Your father is arranging that I buy a plantation in Jamaica," he said to Amanda.

"Where's that?"

"The other side of the world. It might be a charming idea to visit it. Would you like to stay on a sugar plantation for your honeymoon? We could free all the slaves to celebrate our wedding."

"Oh, you do love to talk nonsense." Amanda dimpled at him prettily. "I should hate to leave England."

"Why?"

She gave him a look of pretty impatience at his stupidity. "Because anywhere else is full of foreigners."

"If you are so averse to foreigners, then perhaps you should not meet these Hungarian ladies."

Amanda stamped her foot. "You are tormenting me. You promised!" She actually pronounced it as "pwomised," having a natural lisp rather than a cultivated one like most of her peers, baby talk being all the rage.

"Now, now," admonished her mother. "Lord Eston was only funning. Shall we go?"

"Bless me, here they come," said Cassandra in a gloomy voice. "Lord Eston and the Boyles. What a hairy man Mr. Boyle is, to be sure."

"Look regal," hissed Miss Tonks as the party came up to them.

Lord Eston made the introductions. Miss Tonks inclined her head in a stately way. Cassandra asked them to be seated, covertly studying Amanda. She remembered Lord Eston's story about how a friend of his had made a fool of himself over some chit and now it looked very much as if he had gone and done the same thing himself.

For her part, Amanda was staring at Miss Tonks and Cassandra as if they were exhibits in a menagerie of wild beasts like the one at Exeter 'Change.

"Do you spend long in London, Miss Haldane?" asked Mrs. Boyle.

"I do not know," said Cassandra. "This is not a very good hotel. I have heard the Poor Relation is better."

"You were sadly misinformed," said Mr. Boyle. "The Poor Relation is an uncomfortable place run by seedy people."

Miss Tonks's nose turned pink at the tip. "Lady Fortescue," she said awfully, "is a friend of my . . . family."

There was an embarrassed silence. Then Amanda ventured, "Is Hungary very far away?"

"Quite far," said Cassandra.

"Farther than France?"

"Yes, even farther than Italy."

"And what is it like?"

"I fear our hotelier has been gossiping," said Cassandra. "We prefer to remain incognito. In our exalted position, we have many enemies."

"Oh!" Amanda clasped her hands. "Enemies. Why is that?"

"I see you have a kind face." Cassandra leaned forward. "I was betrothed to a prince. His forebears"—she shuddered delicately—"were Magyars. Fierce and savage people. I shunned him. I said I would never marry him. He said he would force me to the altar. My dear companion and some of our most trusted servants arranged for me to flee the country. But the prince and his henchmen caught up with us at the border."

Lord Eston stifled a groan.

"Goodness!" Amanda was goggling. "What happened then?"

"All our servants were killed. We were bound and taken captive, but on the road, one of the prince's servants took pity on us and released us. We fled on horseback through the night," said Cassandra dreamily. "I can see it all now. The glittering snow, the wolves skulking among the trees, and us flying through the night under a full moon, dreading every moment to be captured again."

There was a long silence. Mr. Boyle was dying to ask this fascinating pair what they did for money.

As if sensing this unspoken question hanging in the air between them, Cassandra gave him a brilliant smile and said, "We were lucky enough to bring a great quantity of fine jewels with us or we should have been destitute. In fact, as we have enough to last us a lifetime, I think we should consider taking a house in Town. With the exception of yourselves"—she smiled sweetly on the Boyles—"there are a great many common people in this hotel, and it does one's social consequence little good to be seen in such a *low* establishment."

"We should leave as well," said Amanda immediately. "I don't want to be unfashionable, Mama."

Mr. and Mrs. Boyle looked uncomfortable and Lord

Eston suspected that they might have obtained free lodging from Bonnard in return for some favour. But what favour? Had Bonnard been offered the corn-thresher or the plantation?

"And now I think we will retire," said Cassandra. She and Miss Tonks rose. Amanda and her mother sank into full court curtsies while the gentlemen bowed.

"Fascinating," breathed Amanda.

"Yes," agreed Lord Eston drily. "Quite fascinating."

In their private hotel sitting-room, Cassandra sank down into a chair and laughed helplessly. "Did you see their faces?" she said when she could.

"I don't know how you think of such things," exclaimed Miss Tonks. "But perhaps you have gone a little far. We shall become an object of curiosity."

"By that time we shall have found out some facts about Bonnard and paid our shot here," said Cassandra blithely.

Miss Tonks looked doubtful. "I cannot help feeling we would have found out more had we masqueraded as servants."

A servant scratched at the door and entered bearing a large basket full of crystallized fruit. "Mr. Bonnard's compliments," he said, "and Mr. Bonnard would be honoured if the ladies could grant him a few moments of their time."

"Certainly," said Cassandra.

"And what is he up to?" she added when the servant had left. "He looks a greedy man and I have seen him gossiping with Boyle."

Miss Tonks's long nose twitched in distress. "I sense danger." She suddenly added with a burst of rare anger, "You should have a gentleman to protect you, Cassandra. What Lord Eston can see in that feather-brained little fool is beyond me."

"She looks vastly pretty and he delights in her," said Cassandra. "They will probably be very happy."

"Shhh," said Miss Tonks. "Here comes Bonnard."

The hotelier bowed his way into the room.

Cassandra sat bolt upright in her chair. She did not ask him to sit down.

"Your Royal Highness," he began.

Cassandra frowned. "I prefer my title to be kept secret, Mr. Bonnard. Miss Haldane will suffice."

"But certainly, Your . . . Miss Haldane. Your English is perfect."

"I had an English governess." Cassandra surveyed Bonnard. "Why is *your* English so perfect?"

"I was born here. My parents fled the Terror."

Cassandra did a quick sum in her head. Bonnard was over forty if he was a day. He could hardly have been born after the French Revolution. Instead she said, "You wished to see us?"

"This is a very delicate matter," he said. "But many foreign ladies who come to London are often anxious to sell jewels and get cheated. I have a good man who gives top prices. Should you wish anything sold discreetly, you have only to ask me."

Gossiping Mr. Boyle, thought Cassandra. "We will let you know. This is quite a new hotel, I believe."

"Yes, Miss Haldane."

"What did you do before you established this hotel?"

He gave a very Gallic shrug and spread out his hands. "Nothing that would interest you."

Cassandra wondered whether to pursue this topic but decided to leave it for the moment. "I believe the Poor Relation, which is also new, to be a good hotel."

"Oh, miss, it is a terrible place. The food is vile and the servants insolent."

"Then why do people stay there?"

"Because it is run by aristos. But after staying there once, they never return."

"I suppose it is in your interest to run down your rival."

"I do not tell the lies, me," he exclaimed. "But I beg you to remember about the jewels. I am always at your service."

He bowed his way out, walking backwards.

Cassandra sat in thought for a few moments after he had left. Then she said, "I would like to get into that office of his." Bonnard had a little office off the entrance hall.

"It is locked," said Miss Tonks. "I mean, I noticed he locks it when he is not using it and puts the key in his pocket."

"Do you know," said Cassandra, "everything in this hotel is shoddy and painted over with gilt to look expensive. It would not surprise me if all the keys to the doors were interchangeable. I suggest we go down in the middle of the night with the key from here and try it in the lock."

"If what he has in that office, which probably includes the money from the hotel, is so important, then it is going to have a special lock."

Cassandra looked stubborn. "Nonetheless, I am going to try. Do not worry, Aunt, I will go myself. This must all be very frightening for you."

But somehow Miss Tonks had come to believe most of the time that she herself had actually held up Honoria's coach. The plaudits of her partners rang in her ears. She craved further admiration, she who had received practically none in the whole of her life. "I will go, too," she said. "We are here to find out about this Bonnard and it is time we made a move." She leaned forward. "It is such a pity that Lord Eston is throwing himself away on that chit. Such parents!"

"He has proposed to her, the engagement is made

official, so there is little he can do about it now," said Cassandra with every appearance of indifference. "Perhaps he is not a man of very strong character. He more or less said that he was made by his tailor." She leaned her chin on her hands, her eyes suddenly dreamy. "I cannot imagine such as he holding up a coach."

Again Miss Tonks experienced a strong urge to tell her the identity of that highwayman, but gratitude to Lord Eston and fear that her niece would be badly shocked kept her quiet. Although Cassandra and her mother had always been at loggerheads for as long as Miss Tonks could remember, the girl would surely be shocked that Miss Tonks could even contemplate robbing her own sister or allowing Lord Eston to do so.

"You should not be thinking about that highwayman," said Miss Tonks with a shudder. "They are not romantic and always of a singularly low type of fellow. Fortunately, unlike those posting-houses and it not being the Season, the hotel is quiet at night. What say you to two in the morning?"

"Excellent, if we don't fall asleep."

They managed to stay awake by the simple expedient of not retiring to bed. They played cards and listened as the sounds of the hotel quietened. Out in the street, the watchman passed by every half-hour, hoarsely calling out the time and the weather. "Do you not think it stupid that Londoners should pay a man to disturb the night every half an hour by telling them the time and the weather?" asked Cassandra. "If one is all that interested in the weather, one can look out of the window; or if one wants to know the time, at the clock."

"My dear," said her aunt, "a great many poor people do not have clocks."

"But all the church bells of London chime the quarter hours and hours with regular monotony!"

"In truth," said Miss Tonks with a sigh, "I have lived so long in Town, I am become so accustomed to the sound of the watch that I never hear him."

"And, talking of time," said Cassandra, laying down her cards, "it is nearly two o'clock and I have just won twenty-four thousand pounds from you."

"I never had any luck at cards," said Miss Tonks, comfortable in the knowledge they had been playing for fictional money. She plucked at the fringed shawl about her shoulders. "I suppose we had better get on with it. What excuse shall we give if we are caught even near the office?"

Cassandra frowned in thought and then her face cleared. "You forget, we are foreigners and therefore given to eccentric whims. The watchman has his uses after all. He has just announced a clear, moonlit night and all's well, so we can say we wished to view the streets of London by moonlight."

"Very neat. Although I confess it causes me some disquiet that you appear to be taking to a life of subterfuge without a qualm, Cassandra."

"Not subterfuge. Expediency. Shall we go?"

They felt their way down the main staircase in the darkness, not wanting to carry candles. Below them, the soft light of an oil-lamp illumined the hall.

They slowly descended further and then stopped at the foot of the stairs. Cassandra put a warning hand on her aunt's arm. "There is someone in the office," she whispered.

Miss Tonks let out a little gasp of relief. "Then we can do nothing just now," she whispered back.

Cassandra leaned over the newel-post and looked at the

office. It had a glass door covered with a curtain but she could make out the shadows of three men.

"I am going to listen and try to hear what they are saying." She moved quietly forward, with the trembling Miss Tonks after her.

"I said I would help and I think my plan is a good one." Mr. Boyle's voice. It had a harsh, grating edge which Cassandra immediately recognized. "Those foreigners have put it into my Amanda's head that this hotel is unfashionable, so to placate her, I said we would all have dinner there tomorrow night. Now do you know what's to be done?"

"Yes, monsieur," came Bonnard's voice. "Will here has just gained employment in the kitchens of the Poor Relation. There's roast haunch of venison on the menu. The roast will be carried up to the dining-room on a covered dish. Will must put the rat under the cover of the dish just before it goes up to the dining-room . . ."

"Won't answer," said a new voice. Will, thought Cassandra. "The chef carries up the main roast to the dining-room door himself, followed by me. It is placed on a carving table on wheels and wheeled in. Sir Philip Sommerville then carves in front of the guests. I'd be caught."

There was a silence and then Mr. Boyle said, "Is the demned roast never left unsupervised?"

Will again. "Only for a moment. Despard places the roast on the carving table outside the dining-room. He goes in and announces the roast is ready. Sir Philip nods, Despard turns and waves, and the whole thing is wheeled in with great ceremony."

"Then you put the rat in the dish then, man!"

"I dare not," said Will. "I'd be seen. And how do I hide a live rat about me person for the whole day?"

"Look, you milksop, I'll do it," said Mr. Boyle. "I'll excuse myself just before the roast is to be served. Wait a bit, isn't it one of those silver servers which slides up at one side, I mean the lid slides up at one side?"

"Yes, sir."

"Well, there you are. You slide up the side away from the dining-room—you can always say you are checking if the meat is hot enough, I pop in the rat and you put down the lid. Over in a trice. You should be grateful to me, Bonnard."

The hotelier's voice sounded a trifle sullen. "Your apartments are not costing you anything, my friend. It is not as if you are helping me for nothing."

The doorknob began to turn and Cassandra grasped her aunt by the arm and urged her back to the staircase. Once safely back in their sitting-room, they looked at each other, wide-eyed.

"We had better get some sleep," said Cassandra firmly, "and then go and warn the others."

"What if we are followed by one of the servants of this hotel?" asked Miss Tonks.

"They have no reason to suspect us, but to put your mind at rest, we will set out on a shopping expedition, and by the time we have been through Exeter 'Change, we will have lost any pursuer."

Shopping in London was the great amusement of the leisured classes. One did not go necessarily to buy anything, but to pass the day, which was why the shop assistants were all men who were employed to cajole and flatter the female shoppers. On the Continent, the assistants were women, for there people went to buy goods. The English believed women had not the patience to cope with the time-wasting foibles of the idle rich. But it still struck Cassandra as strange that so many young men should be employed in London to recommend laces and muslins to the ladies, to assist them in the choice of a gown, to weigh out threads, and to measure ribbons.

It was early in the morning when she and Miss Tonks set out and so it was leisure time for the young men, who, immaculately dressed, with hair powdered to perfection, stood at their shop doors paring their nails and adjusting their cravats.

Many of the shops now had glass windows and some even had plate-glass windows, with the exception of such merchants as the sellers of woollen cloth, who still had their shops open and windowless to the street in the old manner. The upper classes demanded that their fashions were all purchased in the West End. If a lady found out that a pretty cap purchased for her had come from the City in the east, it would be immediately given to her lady's-maid, who, being as high in the instep as her mistress, would promptly give it to the cook, who could be guaranteed not to be so fussy about the cap's pedigree.

Every shop had its inscription above it and the name of the owner, and previous owner if the business had been so long established as to derive a certain degree of respectability from time. Miss Tonks never tired of the London shops. They had been her theatre in the days of her poverty: always something to see or marvel at.

In one window was a huge sturgeon, in another a painted piece of beef swinging in a roaster to exhibit the machine that turned it. The apothecary boasted a window full of bottles of worms collected from human intestines, and every bottle labelled to say to whom the worms had belonged, and testifying to the efficacy of the drug that had removed them. At a bootmaker's, a boot floated in a basin of water so that people might admire its waterproof qualities, and, at the shop next door, the dummy of a small man sported a coat puckered up in folds, and the folds were filled with water to show the coat was proof against wet.

Then, in another shop farther along, Cassandra and Miss Tonks were captivated by a display of exquisite lamps: lamps of alabaster to shed a pearly light, or formed of cut glass to glitter like diamonds in the drawing-room.

They finally made their way to the Strand and to Exeter 'Change. Exeter 'Change was a bazaar, or street of shops under cover, full of very cheap and useful items. Each item was clearly marked with the price and there was no haggling. The stalls were piled high with knick-knacks: walking-sticks, implements for shaving, knives, scissors, watch-chains, purses, and fans. At the far end was a man in splendid costume who was there to encourage people to pay to visit the menagerie of wild animals in the rooms above.

Miss Tonks was happy. How many times had she passed her weary days amid the bustle and friendly noise of this emporium. But Cassandra, little used to Town, began to feel nervous and restless and tired of being jostled and so told the reluctant Miss Tonks rather sharply that no one was following them and they were wasting time.

A thin sleet was beginning to fall when they emerged and so they took a hack to Bond Street.

"I hope they will know what to do," said Cassandra as they walked into the Poor Relation.

And to her surprise, Miss Tonks said comfortably, "Oh, Sir Philip will know what to do. He always does."

Chapter Six

How now! a rat? Dead, for a ducat, dead!
—WILLIAM SHAKESPEARE

"DOES IT need to be such a *very* large rat?" asked Mrs. Boyle anxiously, eyeing the cage her husband had placed before her.

"The larger the better. Finest specimen the rat-catcher could supply."

"You had best hide the creature before Amanda sees it. As far as miss is concerned, we are having a pleasant dinner with Eston. And how will you carry it? You can hardly walk into the Poor Relation bearing a cage."

"I shall wear my brown coat with the deep pockets. A trifle old-fashioned, I admit, but excellent for the purpose. The pockets have huge flaps which should keep the beast secure."

"But it is such a *lively* rat."

"I shall give the beast a dose of laudanum to keep it quiet until we get there."

"Are you sure this is wise? Amanda knows nothing of this, and when a great rat leaps out, she will have hysterics."

"We got her Eston, didn't we, Mrs. Boyle? A few

hysterics won't kill her," said Mr. Boyle heartlessly, conveniently forgetting that Lord Eston had fallen in love with his daughter rather than being coerced into the engagement.

"Better quieten this thing down." Mr. Boyle picked up the cage.

Mrs. Boyle walked through to her daughter's bedroom to find her surrounded by every item of her wardrobe, which was extensive. "I dare not appear unfashionable and be damned as a provincial, Mama," said Amanda. "If only there were time to get something made."

Casting an expert eye over the gowns, Mrs. Boyle said unhesitatingly, "The pale-blue muslin with the gold sprig and the sapphire necklace we gave you on your last birthday. The Juliet cap with the foil flowers. White kid gloves, blue satin shoes. Yes, that's it. Bring out the colour of your eyes."

"You are sure?"

"Oh, yes. Eston will be more in love with you than ever."

Amanda blushed faintly and turned to her maid. "Leave us," she ordered. When the maid had closed the door behind her, Amanda said, "I fear Lord Eston might be quite brutal."

"What can you mean? He appears the perfect gentleman."

"He kissed me yesterday and I didn't like it one little bit!"

Mrs. Boyle looked impatiently at her daughter. "You'll have to tolerate a great deal more than kisses after you are married. Think of the title you will have, the clothes, the jewels. All you need to do is grit your teeth and produce an heir and a spare and then lead your own life."

"I don't want to be kissed," said Amanda stubbornly.

"Fiddlesticks." A look of steel came into Mrs. Boyle's

eyes. "We have invested a great deal of money in you, my pretty, and now it is your duty to pay us back. Have we affianced you to some toad, some hunchback? We have found you a handsome lord, so don't you dare do anything to disaffect him."

Amanda's pug came snorting up to her and she lifted the little dog up. "Rupert loves me. He will bite nasty Lord Eston if he gets too rough. Will you not, my precious?"

"Just behave prettily and leave the rest to me," said her mother.

A council of war had gathered at the Poor Relation. They all listened while Cassandra and Miss Tonks outlined the Plan of the Rat.

"We shall send a man round to Tupple's to say that the Boyles's booking for dinner was a mistake and cancel it," said the colonel.

Sir Philip Sommerville looked at him with contempt. "And let the scoundrel get away unpunished? Let me think. He cannot carry a rat in by the tail, nor can he carry it openly in a cage. So it has to be in a pocket." He narrowed his eyes. "Yes, I think I have a plan."

"Do tell us," said Lady Fortescue. "I must admit you are very clever when it comes to getting us out of predicaments."

The colonel glared.

"First," said Sir Philip, "is we get Despard up here and tell him what is going on. That fellow, Will, must be dismissed. Can't have spies in the kitchen. Our reputation hangs on Despard's cooking."

Soon Despard appeared before them. Cassandra thought he looked villainous. He was a skinny man with a white face and his mouth was twisted up on one side in a perpetual sneer.

"The situation is this," said Sir Philip. "There's a party

by the name of Boyle who will be dining here with Lord Eston. Mr. Boyle is in league with Tupple's. That fellow, Will, you have in your kitchen is a spy for them. Anyway, Boyle plans to pop a rat in with the venison roast tonight just before it is wheeled into the dining-room for me to carve."

"I kill him," said the cook in the same flat indifferent voice in which he discussed the day's menus.

"Here, none of that," exclaimed the colonel, alarmed. "Nor do we want Tupple's to know we are on to them. You just say you don't need him and send him packing."

"But what about this 'ere rat?" demanded Despard, whose French accent was now mixed with broad Cockney.

"I have everything in control," said Sir Philip.

Despard bowed. Sir Philip was the only one he held in respect, Sir Philip having rescued him from the gallows by intervening in his trial at the Old Bailey.

"Why I brought you up here," Sir Philip went on, "was to tell you to get rid of Will. Don't look surprised at anything that might happen when you wheel that venison in."

"Very good, sir."

"That will be all."

"Well, that's that," said Sir Philip when the cook had left. "You ladies had best return to Tupple's and keep up the good work."

"A moment!" Lady Fortescue held up a hand. "You have forgotten something, Sir Philip. Miss Tonks, please wait downstairs. We have something to say to Miss Cassandra."

"Whatever you have to say to my niece, you can say to me." Miss Tonks stood in front of Cassandra and spread out her skirts in a protective gesture.

"Miss Tonks." Lady Fortescue's voice was steely. "I

must insist! You may take Mrs. Budley with you. Miss Cassandra has our permission to tell you of what we have said afterwards if she is so inclined."

"Well . . ."

"Oh, do go along," Cassandra urged her aunt. "I am quite capable of looking after myself."

So Miss Tonks and Mrs. Budley reluctantly left.

Cassandra's eyes roamed from face to face. The colonel's colour was slightly raised and he was looking steadily at the floor; Sir Philip appeared amused. Lady Fortescue's black eyes were steady and concerned.

"You are fond of your aunt, are you not, my dear?"

"Yes, very fond, indeed."

"As are we all." Lady Fortescue hesitated and then went on firmly. "Do you know that there are ladies who prefer their own sex?"

Cassandra looked surprised. "And I am glad of it," she cried. "I have no time for those silly misses who affect to despise their own sex."

"That is not quite what I mean."

Lady Fortescue's eyes flew instinctively to Sir Philip for help, and Colonel Sandhurst could not bear that. "What Lady Fortescue is trying to say," he pointed out gruffly, "is that there are certain females who make love to their own kind."

Cassandra's eyes widened in surprise and Lady Fortescue thought that it might be a good idea if young ladies were given more of a classical education. A classical education made a lot of things clearer. "How odd," said Cassandra. "What has that got to do with me?"

Lady Fortescue took over again. "When that highwayman kissed you, you said you liked it."

Cassandra blushed and laughed. "Yes."

"We have discussed this matter among ourselves and we have come to a decision. We suggest that you ask Miss

Tonks the identity of that highwayman, and as soon as possible."

"But why?"

"Because she knows his identity."

"What! How on earth can she? Aunt Letitia know a highwayman? How ridiculous."

"You will find we are all putting ourselves at peril by suggesting this to you. But you are far from home and parents and it is our duty to take care of you. Pray, I beg you, ask Miss Tonks who that highwayman was."

"Very well," said Cassandra, "but you will find she knows nothing of it."

When Cassandra had left, Sir Philip said waspishly, "I was against this, you know. She will find out her aunt is one of Sappho's daughters and that her aunt stole her mother's jewels and gave them to us. If she tells that dreadful Honoria Blessop, we are lost."

"Should that threat arise," said Lady Fortescue, "then we shall be obliged to tell her that she herself, by virtue of accepting our hospitality, is implicated in the plot. I am glad we sent Mrs. Budley away. Such practices might puzzle her. She is an innocent."

Sir Philip surveyed her with admiration. "You can be quite ruthless when you have to be, dear lady."

"Tcha!" said Colonel Sandhurst.

Miss Tonks eyed her niece uneasily. To questions as to what the others had said to her, Cassandra would only reply, "When we are private."

Reminded of her days at a seminary in Bath when she had to wait for an interview with the principal, Miss Tonks grew increasingly nervous as Tupple's Hotel appeared outside the windows of the hack. Like a guilty schoolgirl she followed her niece indoors and up the stairs. There was an air of suppressed excitement emanating from Cassandra.

She had discounted all those odd remarks about women. The one thought in her mind was that Aunt Letitia must surely know the identity of that highwayman. She had not thought so in the sitting-room of the Poor Relation. But she had come to the conclusion that they must have been telling the truth.

She had never forgotten that kiss. Although the road had been dark, the light from the carriage lamps had given her a view of that smiling mouth and glittering eyes behind a black mask.

"Now, Aunt," she said firmly, "pray be seated. Lady Fortescue and the others assure me that you know the identity of that highwayman."

Startled, Miss Tonks stared at her. Why had the others not told her? What if Cassandra was so furious at the robbery of her mother's jewels that she told all to the authorities? But the cat was well and truly out of the bag.

"Yes," she whispered.

Cassandra's large eyes flashed with triumph. "Who is he?"

Miss Tonks bent her head. "It was I," she said. "We desperately needed money for the hotel. Honoria has kept me on short commons, just above starvation, for years. I shall pay her back, every penny, when we are in funds."

Cassandra's face was blank with shock. "Why . . . why d-did you k-kiss me like that?"

"I was acting out a part," said Miss Tonks wretchedly.

"Lady Fortescue told me that there are ladies such as you," said Cassandra, "who prefer their own sex. But your own niece . . . !"

Miss Tonks began to cry. Cassandra walked to the window and stared down bleakly into the sooty London street. For the first time since her escape, she wanted to go home. She had been sustained in her adventures by the memory of that kiss, had thought she was emulating the highwayman by spying on Tupple's.

"I must tell you the truth," said Miss Tonks in a choked voice.

"I thought you already had." Cassandra continued to look down into the street.

There was a knock at the door and then a servant entered with a card on a tray. "Lord Eston's compliments."

"Not now," said Cassandra curtly. "Tell his lordship we are not at home."

"Stay!" Miss Tonks stood up and firmly dried her eyes. "Tell his lordship we shall be pleased to receive him."

"I know you are distressed and embarrassed, Aunt," said Cassandra in a thin voice, "but hiding behind the company of Lord Eston does not alter matters."

"There is something he must explain," said Miss Tonks.

Lord Eston came in, bowed, and then looked in slight surprise from Miss Tonks's tearful face to Cassandra's hard one. "If I have come at the wrong time . . ." he began.

"No, no," said Miss Tonks. "Pray be seated. My lord, Miss Cassandra asked me the identity of the highwayman who robbed my sister of her jewels. I said it was I."

His eyes began to dance. "How very awkward for you."

"I cannot tell her anything more without your permission. You see, my colleagues believed it to be me and when they found out that this highwayman had kissed my niece, they were naturally concerned."

"I suppose now that Miss Cassandra knows so much, she may as well know all," he said, "and then we must rely on her mercy and understanding."

"The fact is that your aunt meant to hold up her sister's coach, but held up mine by mistake. I offered to do the job

100

for her and I did. I regret, Miss Cassandra, that it was I who kissed you."

Cassandra sat down suddenly. She looked at him as if seeing him for the first time. Her gaze travelled from his guinea-gold hair to the tips of his shiny Hessian boots. "But why did you kiss me?"

"You have a kissable face."

"Oh."

In a voice that tried pathetically not to shake, Miss Tonks said, "Are you going to report us to the authorities?"

Cassandra blinked. "No, of course not," she said. "Mama can well afford to lose the entire contents of her jewel box without it affecting her overmuch. But you should have told me, Aunt." The last sentence came out as a wail. All her dreams of a bold and handsome highwayman gone, crumbled into dust, and her hand brushed across her own mouth as if trying to brush away that kiss.

Lord Eston felt an odd tug at his heart. He was used to a bold and confident Cassandra, but this shocked and disappointed young lady looked so appealing and vulnerable. Besides, there were those freckles and that ridiculous little nose. How odd that such a combination of unfashionable features should appear so endearing. He remembered he had been afraid of falling in love with her and had been glad to escape to the manor-house, and the reason he had been afraid was because he had not considered her very respectable. And yet now he was tied to a future villanous father-in-law and had blithely admitted to the girl that he had stolen her mother's jewels. Who on earth was he to be so high in the instep?

He turned to Miss Tonks. "I gather you did not tell the others that it was I who held up the coach?"

"No, my lord. I could not implicate you."

"Then you have my permission to tell them now."

The end of Miss Tonks's nose turned pink with distress. "I do not want to," she mumbled.

"Why?" asked Cassandra.

"They are so proud of me, even the dreadful Sir Philip."

"Oh, but look how proud they are of you, of both of us, for having found out Mr. Boyle's dreadful plot." Cassandra bit her lip. Lord Eston was staring at her in surprise.

"You had better tell me about this plot."

"I should have held my tongue," said Cassandra. "We overheard Mr. Boyle talking to Bonnard. He plans to take a live rat to the Poor Relation this evening and slip it into the dish containing the haunch of venison before it is taken into the dining-room. That way Bonnard allows him to stay here free."

Lord Eston looked at her bleakly. There was no point in protesting Boyle's innocence. He already knew the man to be a crook. "So what are you going to do?" he asked.

"Sir Philip said he would handle everything," said Miss Tonks, "and he is very clever at things like that."

Lord Eston tried to conjure up a picture of his fiancée's pretty face to console himself, but all he could think of was the perfidy of the family he was about to ally his name with.

"Mr. Davenport," announced a servant from the doorway, and before either Miss Tonks or Cassandra could protest that they did not know any Mr. Davenport, the gentleman himself walked into the room. He was a tall, willowy youth, slightly pock-marked and dressed in the height of fashion: wasp-waisted coat, padded shoulders, striped waistcoat, and hair frizzed up high on his head.

He knelt before Cassandra and presented her with a bouquet of flowers.

"Your Highness," he said, "I have heard of your bravery, your courage. Ah, had I been at your side, we would have fled across the steppes together."

"They didn't come from Russia," said Lord Eston testily. "Do get to your feet, sir, and introduce yourself properly."

The young man stood up and put one hand on his breast. "I am Aubrey Davenport of the Wiltshire Davenports."

Lord Eston smiled and made the introductions, giving Miss Tonks and Cassandra their aliases.

"How did you learn of us?" asked Cassandra.

"I met a certain Mr. Boyle. He confided in me. He assured me you never saw anyone . . ."

"But said he could arrange it with one of the hotel servants to have you ushered directly into the presence," said Lord Eston. "How much?"

"My lord?"

"How much did Boyle charge you?"

"A trifle. A mere five guineas. But what is money?"

"Money is what makes Mr. Boyle go round." Lord Eston got to his feet. "I will take my leave, ladies."

Cassandra felt quite flat after he had gone. It was a pity he had turned out to be her highwayman, but he was a fellow conspirator and it would have been fun to talk to him a little longer and perhaps beg him to call on them after the dinner this evening and give them an account of what had happened.

With a little sigh, she settled down to tell the dazed and admiring Mr. Davenport some highly fanciful tales of her life in Hungary.

Sir Philip was waiting in the hall when the Boyle family and Lord Eston arrived. Inside Mr. Boyle's capacious pocket lay one very dead rat. He had overdone the dose of laudanum, and so the rat, who had lived long and scavenged hard, had departed painlessly to rat heaven on a cloud of opium fumes just as the carriage had drawn up outside the Poor Relation.

"Welcome, welcome," cried Sir Philip. "Faith, sir"—to Mr. Boyle—"there is dust on your coat. Our treacherous streets. Jacky, the brush." A servant ran forward with a large clothes-brush and, to Lord Eston's amusement, Sir Philip began to apply it vigorously to Mr. Boyle's coat.

"No, it will not come off, sir. See, there, it is stained with soot," said Sir Philip, and so it was, the brush having been dusted with soot before it had been applied to Mr. Boyle's coat. "Jacky, take this gentleman's coat to the kitchens. No, but a trice, sir. A trice."

"I am not going to stand here without my coat," howled Mr. Boyle, turning red.

"Papa," said Amanda, casting an agonized look about the splendour of the entrance hall. "Do not make a scene."

Mr. Boyle reluctantly surrendered his coat. They would hardly search the pockets! But he waited in an agony of suspense until the coat, cleaned and brushed, was returned to him. With relief, he felt the comforting weight still in that pocket.

They were ushered into the dining-room. Sir Philip, who appeared to have been taking snuff while waiting for the coat to reappear and had been waving the silver box around in an exaggerated manner, closed it with a snap.

Amanda looked about her. Everyone looked extremely prosperous and elegant. As they ate their way through the soup and fish courses, Lord Eston wondered what was going to happen about that rat.

His hair was beginning to itch and that was distracting his thoughts. His valet had used a new pomade. He must tell him to throw it out. He wished he did not have to be so polite and could give his head a good scratch.

Then, as Sir Philip, standing by the sideboard, began to

sharpen the carving knife, Mr. Boyle muttered an excuse, got to his feet and went out.

To his dismay, it was not Will standing with Despard beside the huge serving tray with its silver cover but another servant. He smiled weakly at them. "Must get a little fresh air," he said, moving a few feet towards the street door.

Despard walked into the dining-room and announced the roast. Mr. Boyle swung round and said to the servant, "Be a good fellow and have a look over there by the door. I think I've lost my stick-pin." And when the servant had left, Mr. Boyle whipped up the cover, unbuttoned the flap of his pocket and dived a hand in.

Then he let out a scream of pain.

The diners, led by Lord Eston, crowded in the entrance to the hall from the dining-room. Mr. Boyle was doing a sort of war-dance, with a large rat-trap clamped round one hand.

Sir Philip pushed his way through watching guests. "You are creating a disturbance," he said severely.

"Where did this come from?" howled Mr. Boyle.

"From your own coat," said the servant, who had pretended to look for that mythical stick-pin.

Mr. Boyle was in an agony of pain and rage. Lord Eston sprang the trap and examined his fingers. "Not broken," he said, "but they will be very stiff and painful."

"Would you please return to your places," said a voice, awful in its majesty. Lady Fortescue had arrived.

Meekly they all filed back in, Lord Eston surreptitiously scratching his head.

Once they were seated, he noticed Amanda wincing and rubbing at her hair with her fan. Mrs. Boyle's face was covered in a light sheen of sweat.

And then Lady Fortescue, dressed in severe black, with her white hair under a snowy cap, bore down on them.

Her voice carried round the dining-room. "I must ask you all to leave."

"Why?" demanded Lord Eston.

"You should know why, but you force me to point out that all of you are covered in head lice. So badly, that some are visible on Miss Boyle's neck."

Amanda screamed and tore at her hair and then fell sobbing on the floor.

"You tricked me," howled Mr. Boyle, glaring at Sir Philip.

"Please," said Sir Philip, waving a scented handkerchief. "Please go before you infest our guests."

Mr. Boyle could not elaborate on his accusations without betraying that he had planned to ruin the hotel.

Lord Eston carried his weeping fiancée out. Her eyes were red and puffy and he fought down a feeling of impatience with her. He was furious with Miss Tonks and Cassandra. They must have known what the plot was and they should have warned him.

"How did you manage it?" whispered Lady Fortescue when the disgraced party had left. Sir Philip drew a silver box from his pocket. "A lice box, dear lady."

Lady Fortescue was startled into a surprisingly girlish giggle. "You *dreadful* man."

It had been the custom early in the last century for fashionables to carry lice boxes, it being considered bad-mannered to kill your louse and stamp on it on your hostess's carpet. Much politer to pop it in a box and take it home, to be discreetly put to death. The idea had come to Sir Philip earlier in the day when he had gone down to the kitchens to find Despard shaving the head of the pot-boy because the lad's head had been infested with lice. Sir Philip had collected enough lice to wave around the Boyle party when they arrived in the hall.

✱   ✱   ✱

Much as Lord Eston wanted to go straight to Tupple's and confront Cassandra, he had to be deloused first, and that was a long process. First his valet had to prepare a mixture of five parts of sabadilla seed, five parts alcohol, nine parts acetic acid, and thirty-six parts of water. The resulting mixture was combed through Lord Eston's hair and then his head was bound up in a white cloth. This had to be left on all night and then his hair washed thoroughly in the morning and combed with a fine-toothed comb. The clothes he had been wearing the night before he gave to his valet to dispose of. Finally, curled and barbered, he set out at noon for Tupple's Hotel, his head still sore from all the combing and washing.

The day was fine and the sun was shining—although shining down through the pall of smoke that always covered London and hung about the corners of the streets, making the most ordinary thoroughfare look mysterious. London was busy with buying and selling. Shops everywhere, miles of them, a shop to every house: drapers, stationers, confectioners, pastry cooks, seal-cutters, silversmiths, booksellers, print sellers, hosiers, fruiterers, and china warehouses. And where there was a vacant house or a temporary scaffolding erected for repairs, every available space was plastered with advertisements. As he walked along Oxford Street, two rival blacking-makers were competing with each other. Each carried a boot, completely varnished with black, hanging from a pole, and, on another arm, the balls of blacking for sale. On the top of the poles they carried was a sort of standard explaining the virtue of the wares. The one said that his blacking was the best blacking in the world; the other, that his was so good you could eat it.

Conscious of his clean gloves, Lord Eston avoided outstretched offers of playbills; the ink was always wet from the printer.

The walk had put him in a slightly better frame of mind. Duty made him send his respects to the Boyles first and ask to see Amanda, but he was told by a surly Mr. Boyle that Miss Amanda was overset and not able to see anyone.

He went straight to Cassandra's apartments and announced himself.

Cassandra was alone in the sitting-room. Her face lit up when she saw him and he felt a queer tug at his heart and had to remind himself severely that he was angry with her and proceeded to say so . . . at length, describing the events of the night before.

She heard him out in a composed way and then she began to laugh, as heartily as an apple woman, until tears were streaming down her face.

"Do you not see how *funny* it all is?" she gasped finally. "But Miss Tonks and I are all set for this evening." She went to a cupboard in the corner of the room and from the bottom of it drew out a dead cat and held it up. "See," she said, her eyes dancing. "There is roast mutton tonight . . . *au chat!*"

"You hoyden! When that dead cat appears in his dining-room, Bonnard is going to look hard at his supposed Hungarians. Has he not wondered at your lack of servants?"

"Of course. But you forget, they were all killed by the wicked prince and we distrust English ones."

"You are getting deeper and deeper into trouble. Your behaviour is reprehensible."

"*My* behaviour? *I* do not go around holding up coaches and robbing people."

At that moment the door opened quietly and Amanda slipped in. The smile faded from her face when she saw Lord Eston.

"I was told you could not see me," said Lord Eston harshly.

"I wanted to get away from my parents for a little," said Amanda, hanging her head.

"Come and sit down," said Cassandra quickly. "Lord Eston has just been telling me of your terrible ordeal at the Poor Relation."

"Oh, awful. The shame of it. Not to mention all the tiresome scrubbing and delousing," added Amanda in a more practical voice.

"Mr. Aubrey Davenport," announced a hotel servant.

"Is the whole of London to call on you?" muttered Lord Eston.

Mr. Davenport came in bearing a huge bunch of hot-house flowers. He moved towards Cassandra, and then his eyes fell on Amanda and he stopped short and stared at her in a dazed way.

Amanda blushed and dimpled. Like a sleep-walker, Mr. Davenport held out the bouquet to Amanda.

She took it and said, "How delightful."

"My love," said Lord Eston sharply, "as you have not been introduced to this gentleman, you should understand the flowers are for Miss Ca— Miss Haldane."

"That is quite all right," said Cassandra quickly. Amanda threw Lord Eston a rather sulky look and tightened her grasp on the bouquet.

Mr. Davenport recollected himself. "I came, Miss Haldane," he said, "to beg you to take the air with me."

"A drive? I am afraid not, Mr. Davenport," said Cassandra.

"I have recently purchased a high-perch phaeton."

"Ooh," said Amanda. "Is it very high?"

"Very high, Miss . . . ?"

"Boyle. Amanda Boyle." Amanda put down the bouquet and held out one little white hand, which he gallantly kissed.

A dreamy look came into Amanda's eyes. "I have a new bonnet," she said. "A lady in a new bonnet on a high-perch phaeton would be admired by all."

"Then, as Miss Haldane is unable to accept my offer, perhaps . . . ?"

"Miss Boyle is my fiancée," said Lord Eston harshly.

Amanda appeared to have been suddenly struck deaf as far as he was concerned.

"You had better come and meet my parents, Mr. Davenport," she said. "You must obtain their permission." She picked up the bouquet and tripped from the room without a backward glance. Mr. Davenport gave a jerky little bow in Cassandra's direction and hurried after Amanda.

"I'd better put a stop to this." Lord Eston made to follow them out.

"You look stuffy and angry, quite like the heavy father and not like a man who could play highwayman," said Cassandra on a gurgle of laughter. "Oh, run along, do, but mark my words: outrage does not become you."

"You had better put that dead cat away," he retorted nastily. "Do you know you left it in full view?"

"How silly of me." She put the cat away. Something prompted her to add maliciously, "I do not think Mr. Davenport and Miss Boyle had eyes for anything other than each other."

He seized her by her shoulders and gave her a shake and then immediately released her. "You minx! You taunted me into misbehaving myself. You will not see me again."

"I should not have made that remark," she said contritely. She looked up into his face, appeal in her eyes. "I am sadly blunt, you know that, my lord. Please forgive me."

His face relaxed. "Yes, of course I forgive you. But I

wish I had never let Miss Tonks embroil me in her mad schemes. I wish . . ."

He broke off.

"You were about to say you wished you had never kissed me!"

"I . . ."

"Pooh! Think nothing of it. It meant nothing to me." But it had meant a lot, thought Cassandra, it had meant a rosy dream of love and romance, now shattered. To her horror, she could feel tears welling up in her eyes.

"Why, Cassandra!" he said.

He bent his head and kissed her. He could taste the salt from her tears, then the warmth of her lips, sweet and yearning against his own. He could feel the heat and vitality of the pliant body against his own, the swell of her breasts against his chest. London seemed to have fallen silent in that moment. No street cries, no traffic. A magic world of silence, of sweetness, a coming home after a long hard journey.

In the bedchamber next door, Miss Tonks suddenly coughed. He broke away from Cassandra.

"I do not know why I did that," he said huskily.

Cassandra's eyes were enormous in her pale face. "I do."

"Why, Lord Eston!" Miss Tonks came into the room. "Such a long sleep! Cassandra, what are you thinking of? No refreshments? Tea, my lord, or some wine, although it is my belief that Bonnard waters it."

"No, no, I must leave," said Lord Eston. He must return at some point and explain his outrageous behaviour to Cassandra. Yes, that was it.

"I am dining here with the Boyles this evening," he said. "I shall see you then. Perhaps you would both care to join us?"

"We cannot do that," said Miss Tonks. "Such an adventure. We are going to have a dead cat put in with the mutton roast. Such a horrible specimen, too. Do show his lordship the cat, Cassandra."

"I have already seen the cat," said Lord Eston, "and I think it is all a mad, bad, and dangerous idea. You will draw Bonnard's attention to yourselves. Good day, ladies."

"Do you know," said Miss Tonks after he had closed the door behind him, "I really do not think his engagement suits him. He is becoming quite old and pompous."

To Lord Eston's dismay, Mr. Davenport was also a guest at the dinner table that evening. It transpired he had offered to buy the Jamaican plantation. Lord Eston, who thought Davenport had an infernal cheek in the way he was courting Amanda, decided to let him be gulled by Boyle. He deserved it. He had made inquiries about this Davenport and found to his surprise that the young man was extremely rich, having inherited several estates and coal-mines from his father.

Lord Eston glanced around the dining-room. Cassandra and Miss Tonks were there. Miss Tonks still sported that dreadful blond wig and her cheeks still bulged with wax-pads. He wondered how she managed to eat. Then he remembered that it was only recently that the Dutch-doll look had been in fashion and quite a number of women had worn wax-pads to plump out their cheeks and yet had managed to appear to eat quite comfortably.

Cassandra still looked paler than usual, and he assumed his kiss had upset her and came more than ever determined to explain himself, although he did not yet know what kind of explanation he could give.

But there was another reason for Cassandra's pallor. She and Miss Tonks had gone out that afternoon with the dead cat and had given it to Sir Philip, who had said he had everything arranged. On their return, Cassandra became sure their rooms had been searched. She was very precise about laying out her toilet-things and she knew they had been moved. The investigation of Bonnard was not very funny anymore. Cassandra wanted a strong shoulder to lean on, but Lord Eston's strong shoulders were both at another table where he was dining with his pretty fiancée.

"Have you an interest in sugar plantations?" Lord Eston was asking Mr. Davenport. "None at all," said the young man in a vague, light voice.

Lord Eston had decided to leave the matter of the sugar plantation alone, but his conscience was beginning to nag him.

"Then how will you run it?"

"I won't," said Mr. Davenport. He suddenly smiled at Amanda, who smiled back and then raised her fan to cover her blushes. "Mr. Boyle will."

"Here!" Mr. Boyle looked alarmed. "I'm only arranging the sale."

"Yes, but you told me you knew all about the business," said Mr. Davenport patiently, "and I don't know anything, so I've decided to send you out there to handle it all."

"I can't go. My daughter's getting married."

"After the wedding."

Lord Eston thought he could practically see the wheels and cogs of Mr. Boyle's busy brain revolving behind his eyes.

"Very well, then," he said. "You put up the money first and I'll secure the lands and property for you."

"I hoped you would say that. I will give you the money when you leave, and the same sum again to act as my agent. You will remain in Jamaica, with Mrs. Boyle, of course, for the period of three years, and you will therefore be able to send me frequent bulletins."

Mr. Boyle sat deep in thought. It was an enormous sum

this young man was offering. Vast. More money than he had tricked out of anyone in the whole of his life. He could take the money and go. Stick it out for a year and then write and say that the whole venture had collapsed due to flood, hurricane, and famine, and that he himself was ruined. Then he and Mrs. Boyle could return and demand that this young man recompense them for their time and trouble and hardship. Brilliant, he thought, half closing his eyes.

"Yes, all right, young man," he said, opening his eyes to their fullest. Mr. Boyle then glanced at Lord Eston, who was looking edgy and not his usual urbane self. How tiresome he had turned out to be, and not any little bit as gullible as he had imagined. Now Bonnard had told him only that afternoon, when Amanda had gone out driving with Davenport, that Aubrey Davenport was reckoned to be one of the richest men in England. Eston had a title, but he had shown a nasty shrewd streak when it came to parting with money. When Amanda had introduced Davenport that afternoon, Mr. Boyle had promptly suggested the plantation deal and had been delighted when Davenport had appeared to take the bait.

What with planning with Bonnard the downfall of the Poor Relation, Mr. Boyle had not had any time to urge his wife into being sweet to her dying sister, Mrs. Sinclair. He began to feel overworked and ill done by.

At the door to the dining-room stood Bonnard, resplendent in evening dress. He snapped his fingers and the joint was wheeled in in its covered dish.

Lord Eston saw Cassandra grow tense.

With a flourish, Bonnard removed the silver cover. And there, in all its glory, was a beautifully cooked, elegantly dressed leg of mutton.

"No cat," murmured Cassandra.

"Dear me," said Miss Tonks. "It is the first time, I think, that I have ever known Sir Philip to fail."

Lord Eston himself relaxed and began to flirt with Amanda. But to his annoyance she kept throwing him scared little looks and then glancing sideways out of the corner of her eyes to see if Mr. Davenport had noticed.

Miss Tonks did not like to tell Cassandra that she was actually glad Sir Philip's plan had failed. She settled down to enjoy her dinner, her enjoyment sharpened by the recent memory of hungry days.

There were some distinguished guests in the dining-room that evening. There was old Lady Rumbelow with her daughter, Mrs. Trust, and her granddaughter, Fanny.

"I wonder when my sister will get in touch with you," said Miss Tonks to Cassandra.

"Mama already has."

"How so? When?"

"She sent a letter to the Poor Relation and a page brought it round."

"Mercy! One of the pages from the Poor Relation! My dear, what if the boy was recognized?"

"He was in plain livery and one small page looks much like another."

"So what did Honoria say?"

"She said she would give me a month to realize the depths to which I had sunk and then she and Papa would fetch me and take me to that seminary. Mama says by that time I should be begging her to be taken away."

"Foolish woman." Miss Tonks shook her head and they finished their mutton in silence.

After the plates had been cleared away, Bonnard stood proudly in the middle of the room and raised his arms.

"My lord, ladies and gentlemen," he announced. "I have engaged the services of the royal confectioner to create a delicacy for you. See!"

He pointed triumphantly to the door.

A small table on wheels moved slowly into the centre of the room, pushed by two waiters. On it stood a sugar lion, a magnificent beast with snarling jaws and one paw raised. Beside him stood a palm tree with a toffee trunk and green spun-sugar leaves.

Everyone clapped. It was a stupendous creation.

Another table with plates was brought up next to it. A waiter handed Bonnard a long silver knife. He turned and bowed low before old Lady Rumbelow and held the knife out like a ceremonial sword.

"Will your ladyship do my humble hotel the honour of making the first cut?"

"Do it yourself, man," said Lady Rumbelow.

"Let me!" cried Fanny Trust.

Amanda Boyle rose and went over to the sugar lion. "You are not resident here," she said to Fanny. "I am. *I* should have the honour of cutting the lion."

"Ladies, ladies," pleaded Bonnard.

But Lady Rumbelow settled the matter. "Sit down again, Fanny, and stop making a cake of yourself."

Fanny flounced back into her seat.

With a triumphant look all round, Amanda seized the long thin knife and slashed down on the lion's back.

She stood and stared.

Sticky dark-red blood was oozing down over the white sugar, tufts of mangy fur seemed to sprout suddenly from the lion's back.

Lord Eston went over and picked up a heavy silver spoon and brought it smartly down on the lion's head. Pieces of spun sugar flew about, a cloud of sugar dust rose to the chandelier.

And there, revealed to all, was the dead and mangy head of a cat.

Amanda began to scream. Fanny Trust, not to be out-done in sensibility, began to scream as well.

Lord Eston looked at Cassandra.

Cassandra had a feeling that he might betray her, that he might think the poor relations had gone too far.

She rose to her feet and addressed Miss Tonks in a loud voice, "Come, let us quit this squalid hotel. Mr. Bonnard, we leave in the morning."

And with Miss Tonks scurrying behind her, she made a magnificent exit.

Chapter Seven

Envy, hatred, and malice, and all
uncharitableness.
—THE BOOK OF COMMON PRAYER

"SO YOU'VE come back to us." Sir Philip squinted in the
candle-light at Cassandra and Miss Tonks. "You could
have done more."

"I doubt it," said Cassandra. "Someone had been
searching our rooms." It was the evening following the
cat-dinner. "The story is in the newspapers this morning.
How did you persuade the royal confectioner to make such
a disgusting object?"

"Disgusting be demned. That was a work of art. Despard spent all day on it. Sent a scruffy man round to the
kitchen door to imply he had stolen it from the kitchens of
his master and would let it go for a crown. Bonnard
snapped it up, like the greedy fool he is."

"I think you went too far," ventured Miss Tonks
bravely. "I felt quite ill."

"Oh, my, my, my," jeered Sir Philip. "What nicety!
What sensibility! And yet I suppose you two ladies drove
into London under the bodies rotting on the gibbets without a second look."

Horrible man, thought Cassandra, yet knowing Sir Philip spoke the truth.

"I have found out the identity of that highwayman," said Cassandra.

Mrs. Budley, who had been sitting a little apart, stitching at the hem of a handkerchief, looked up and blushed.

"It was Lord Eston!"

All, with the exception of Miss Tonks, looked in amazement at Cassandra.

"Eston?" barked the colonel. "What's he got to do with it?"

In a halting voice, Miss Tonks told them the truth. Sir Philip began to dance about the room. "Oh, wondrous," he cried. "How prime. If by any chance we're caught out, it will be up to Eston to bail us out."

"You should have told the truth in the first place, Miss Tonks," said Lady Fortescue.

"But I *was* brave. It was my idea to hold up the coach," gasped Miss Tonks. "You're always jeering and laughing at me, Sir Philip, and it's past bearing."

"Here now." Sir Philip stopped in mid-pirouette and knelt down in front of Miss Tonks and took her hand in his. "I'm a waspish old fellow and you're such a sheep, you ask for insults. But you were brave and, demme, now I look at you, you've changed into a fashionable lady of the ton. Dear me, Miss Tonks, we'll need to put a guard on you, or we'll be beating the fellows off with clubs."

"This calls for champagne," said the colonel. "Tell John to bring up a bottle of the best, Betty."

They were like a family, thought Cassandra, when they were all sitting around, drinking champagne. Aloud, she said, "So what happens now?"

"I think we can rest on our laurels," said Lady Fortescue. "Tupple's is trounced. Ours is now undisputedly the finest hotel in London. We are placing an advertisement in the newspapers to the effect that we are closing for the month of February. We shall have the best beds put in and the old ones sold off. They all have old-fashioned brocade hangings, so insanitary, and linen is all the crack now, and mahogany posts."

"Won't . . . won't that cost a great deal of money?" asked Miss Tonks, who still had hopes of sending her sister the money for the jewels.

"Thanks to you, or Lord Eston, we do have a great deal of money," said Lady Fortescue. Miss Tonks twitched uneasily. When Harriet James had been with them, she had kept the books, and kept a check on the money. She had shopped at the cheapest markets early in the morning for produce. For a confessed republican, Despard had paradoxically extravagant ways and preferred to spend money on the best ingredients and have them delivered.

Mrs. Budley, delighted now that she could feel at ease with her friend again, suggested she take Miss Tonks round the hotel to show her the improvements that had already been made. Miss Tonks trailed after her, noticing all the new crystal and fine bone china in the dining-room, the new Turkey red carpet on the stairs, and was glad they could not go into the bedrooms to see what had been done there, because the sight of so much profligate expenditure was making her decidedly uneasy. Her worry increased later that evening when Lady Fortescue took her aside and gave her a large sum of money to buy new clothes. Sir Philip and the colonel were already sporting new coats of the finest tailoring and Lady Fortescue was not in her customary black but in a scarlet-and-white merino gown.

As she lay in bed that night next to Mrs. Budley, Miss Tonks said, "Eliza, I cannot help thinking that the money for the sale of the diamonds is not going to last very long. With the war going on, prices of everything are dreadful. And we are burning beeswax candles, not tallow. Whoever heard of an hotel with beeswax candles? We could have shared out that money and perhaps . . . I have not suggested this before . . . perhaps you and I, Eliza, could take a small and modest lodging somewhere."

But there is a difference between forty, Miss Tonks, and thirty, Mrs. Budley, and Mrs. Budley still dreamt of marrying again.

"Everything will be all right," she said sleepily. "We have survived this far."

Miss Tonks sighed. "And there's Cassandra. Too fine a girl to be locked up in that dreadful seminary. I had hoped . . ."

"Hoped what?"

"Lord Eston seemed quite taken with her. But men are so stupid, so incalculable. Why did he get engaged to an empty-headed little nobody like Amanda Boyle?"

"Men like empty-headed nobodies, Letitia." Mrs. Budley giggled. "There is hope for me yet!"

Lord Eston, while the poor relations slept, was being entertained by the Boyles at Tupple's. He had taken them to his box at the opera and to the ball afterwards. The fact that Mr. Boyle had seen fit to ask Aubrey Davenport as well had not pleased him.

Their desultory conversation was interrupted by a knock at the door and then Bonnard walked in. "A word with you in private, Mr. Boyle," he said.

Mr. Boyle went out with him and was away about half an hour, finally returning in a high state of rage. Bonnard had accused him of being a parasite and had told him that either he packed his bags and left, or paid his bill.

Not wanting to let either Lord Eston or Mr. Davenport know he had been living free, Mr. Boyle started by ranting against Bonnard and saying he would walk out but that they had nowhere to go. Then he turned to Lord Eston and said, "I have just remembered. You were kind enough to offer us the hospitality of your town house. We are delighted to accept."

But Lord Eston thought immediately of all his fine books and art treasures. He thought of returning home one night and finding his home stripped and the lying Mr. Boyle blaming it on some mythical burglars.

"I regret my house is being decorated at the moment," he said.

"That's all right," said Mr. Boyle cheerfully. "Smell of paint never bothered us."

"Not only the decorators but the builders as well," said Lord Eston firmly.

"If I may be of service." Mr. Davenport looked around. "You are welcome to my modest home. My aunt is in residence, and with the presence of Mrs. Boyle, all would be respectable."

"That is vewy good of you," lisped Amanda. Why did she have to say "vewy"? thought Lord Eston.

He and Mr. Davenport left together. "It is time we talked," said Lord Eston.

"By all means." Mr. Davenport fell into step beside him. "I will have my man follow your carriage."

At Lord Eston's house, he led Mr. Davenport into the library and offered him wine and then settled down to get rid of what was annoying him.

"Mr. Davenport, you seem blissfully unaware of the fact that it is I who is to marry Miss Boyle and not you."

"You must forgive me," said the young man, looking not in the slightest put out. "I worship from afar."

"Not far enough."

"Alas, what else could I do? The Boyles had to have somewhere to stay and I could not bear the sight of beauty in distress. But you claim the prize, Lord Eston. All I can hope for is an invitation to your wedding. I beg your forgiveness. I did not mean to upset you by my behaviour. But may I point out, my lord, that for a man in love—and it must be love, for the Boyles are not wealthy—you often do not appear to approve of your fiancée. She was talking to her mother during the opera and you told her sharply to be quiet."

"But I am an oddity. I go to the opera to hear the music."

"How strange."

Lord Eston eyed him narrowly. Aubrey Davenport was dressed like a fop, had the manners of a fop, and appeared to have the intelligence of a potato. Still . . .

"The reason I did not invite the Boyles to stay here is because my future father-in-law may prove to be a trifle light-fingered. Pray, be on your guard."

"After the episode of the cat, I felt sure the Boyles would wish to leave the hotel and I have already put all my valuables in storage." Mr. Davenport gave Lord Eston a limpid gaze.

"So you know about Boyle! Why on earth did you agree to buy that plantation, which I doubt even exists?"

Mr. Davenport lowered his pale eyelashes. "I did it to please Miss Boyle," he murmured.

"As you have given me your apologies, I feel obliged to point out that there is more than likely no Heatherington plantation there."

"My man of business—shrewd chap—pointed out the same thing. Business does muddle my head so. I was quite angry and I do not like being angry. So I am purchasing a small and run-down plantation for very little money on the understanding it will be renamed Heatherington's by the time Mr. Boyle arrives. The present overseer will have instructions to meet the ship and start Mr. Boyle on his duties. That should keep him away for some time."

"But he will simply board the next ship home!"

"I am getting him to sign papers binding him to the job of estates manager."

"How very clever of you," said Lord Eston faintly.

"I am not clever at all. I wanted revenge, so I asked my very knowing man of business how to go about it."

Lord Eston eyed him narrowly. "And just what do you get out of all this?"

"I told you. Revenge. I am very rich and am tired of being treated like a flat. Some fellow once sold me a hunting-box in Yorkshire which turned out to be a fiction. After that, I turned all business arrangements over to the experts."

"Some would think exposing Boyle's perfidy revenge enough."

"Not for me." Mr. Davenport studied his polished fingernails. "I decided to go even further."

"How?" asked Lord Eston, beginning to study him with horrified fascination.

"They are desirous of a reconciliation with Mrs. Boyle's sister, Mrs. Sinclair, a rich widow who lives in Green Street. Mrs. Sinclair is, or was, at death's door. I found she was being waited on by a quack and sent a good physician who prescribed diet and rest and no bleeding. The lady was weak with overmuch bleeding. She left today, with the good physician's instructions, to take the waters in Bath and recuperate. When the Boyles call at Green Street, they will find no one at home."

"You make a bad enemy, sir."

"I think I have been extremely kind and fair, considering the wrong done me." He rose to go. "While Miss Boyle is under my roof, Lord Eston, my house is yours. The . . . er . . . Hungarian ladies have left?"

"I believe so."

"Such courage and gallantry. One would almost suppose them to be English."

"Other races, sir, are equally courageous and gallant."

"I suppose so, my lord. Good night. Your servant at all times."

Lord Eston sat for a long time before the dying fire, thinking things over. He was perfectly sure that Mr. Davenport wished to take Amanda away from him. And he had gone to such efforts to get her parents out of the country and keep them away for some time so that his—hopefully—future in-laws would not be around to plague him.

So why was he, Eston, not furious? Why was he letting Davenport take Amanda under his roof?

He shifted uneasily. He had thought himself deeply in love with Amanda. He realized bleakly that he had been infatuated with her, and that infatuation had disappeared the minute he had held Cassandra in his arms and kissed her for the second time. But he had a shrewd idea that Boyle wanted his daughter to have a title. He had proposed, the engagement had been published, and there was no escape unless Amanda decided to release him.

A long and weary time passed for Cassandra. Her mother and father had called and had been firmly told that no one at the Poor Relation Hotel knew where she or Miss Tonks had gone. When she looked down from an upstairs window and saw her father's bowed shoulders as he left the hotel, she had an impulse to run downstairs and cry out to him. But dread of that seminary kept her where she was.

Her duties at the hotel were light. She was expected to stand in for any servant who fell ill, to arrange flowers in all the rooms, and to mend sheets and curtains.

Lord Eston had not called, and his absence was making Cassandra feel quite bitter about him. He had kissed her while engaged to another, because he thought of her as a sort of upper servant, someone he could take liberties with.

The winter was freezing. Her stone water-bottle exploded with the cold. Frost flowers rimed the windows of her small, cell-like room.

Miss Tonks was feeling very low as well. She had timidly put forward the idea that some of the money for the diamonds might be used to bring Cassandra out at the Season, but Lady Fortescue had said roundly that was sheer folly. Any man interested in Cassandra would soon find out her background and shy away.

And when Miss Tonks had suggested that a gentleman might be so in love with Cassandra that her connection with the hotel would not matter, Lady Fortescue had snorted and said, "Such things only happen in books or to raving beauties, and Cassandra Blessop has no claim to beauty at all." Lady Fortescue actually thought Cassandra quite an attractive girl, but she was exasperated with Miss Tonks. Cassandra, about to enter the "staff" sitting-room, heard Lady Fortescue's remark about her and felt lower in spirits than ever.

One morning, when the hotel finally closed in February, Cassandra went out with Miss Tonks to look at the shops. As they were leaving the hotel, Cassandra saw Mr. Davenport driving past in his carriage, and she swung round with her back to the street. He would surely not recognize Miss Tonks without blond wig and wax-pads. But Cassandra could only pray he had not seen her.

She would have been surprised to learn that Lord Eston was as gloomy as she was herself. Contrary to his expectations, Mr. Davenport behaved like a perfect gentleman and no longer flirted with Amanda or paid her any compliments. Worse than that, Amanda seemed to be looking forward to her wedding, spending most of the time studying patterns of wedding dresses. It did not dawn on him that because he no longer tried to kiss her or even to hold her hand, Amanda had decided he would make a very suitable husband after all. Lord Eston had always assumed that he was pursued by females wherever he went because of his wealth and title, for he was not vain. Amanda knew her fiancé was the handsomest man in London and therefore she herself was a great object of envy. The colder Lord Eston became towards her, the happier she was. She no longer feared his embraces, for there were none to fear. Life as a pretty young bride with plenty of money for gowns and jewels stretched out in front of her.

Mr. Davenport puzzled over the problem. He had at first been sure that Amanda preferred him. He had not thought he would have to insult Lord Eston by pursuing the girl. He had expected her to walk into his arms. In order to find an answer to this puzzling problem, he invented a mythical friend who was about to get married, but who never even courted his love, who never pressed her hand, and yet wondered why the love in question should grow warmer as her swain grew colder.

As a great number of his friends were not particularly bright, devoting what wits they had to the cut of their coats, he was beginning to despair of getting any light thrown on the matter until he remembered his business adviser, Mr. Glennon.

It was worth a try, although he doubted whether Mr. Glennon would know anything about the fair sex. Mr. Glennon, he felt, had never been young but had sprung from his father's head complete with bag-wig and long-tailed coat.

Mr. Glennon, in his dusty office in Lincoln's Inn Fields, gravely heard him out. "Don't suppose you've got a clue either," finished Mr. Davenport.

"I would not say that, sir. The fact is that many young ladies know very little of the intimacies of marriage and therefore are frightened of them. Now that your friend has turned cold, his lady feels secure and unthreatened."

"You're a downy one. Demme, how'd you know that?"

"I am a great observer. On the other hand, it is a pity this friend of yours does not fancy someone else."

"And why is that?"

"Because you wish Miss Boyle for yourself."

Mr. Davenport sat with his mouth open.

"It was easy to guess," said Mr. Glennon. "You buy a useless plantation in Jamaica and get a legal document drawn up for Mr. Boyle to sign binding him to run said estate, that estate to be now named Heatherington's. You admitted you had already paid out a great deal of money to this Boyle for an estate called Heatherington's, which you believe does not exist. Now this story. Amanda Boyle is engaged to Lord Eston. Is there any hope of throwing another charmer in Lord Eston's direction?"

Mr. Davenport shook his head gloomily. "There was some Hungarian lady staying at Tupple's and I could swear Eston was vastly taken with her, but she disappeared."

Mr. Glennon leaned back in his chair and studied the cobwebs on the ceiling. "You could perhaps tell Miss Boyle that Eston is a very lusty man who is holding his carnal desires in check—until after the wedding. Hint at exhausted mistresses who could not sate his desire. If necessary, hint at darker lusts of the soul. All is fair in love and war. Also, try to find where this Hungarian lady has gone. I remember you mentioned her—a Miss Haldane, I believe?—and I took the liberty of studying her when she left Tupple's one day. Somehow, she looked like a typical Englishwoman. Her clothes were English and her companion was wearing a stage wig. I followed them for some time. They went to Exeter 'Change and then took a hack, alighting at the Poor Relation Hotel. They went in and went straight up the stairs as if resident. Everyone knows Tupple's and the Poor Relation are rivals. That same evening, the affair of the cat nearly ruins Tupple's, and the very next day, the mysterious Hungarian ladies disappear. I think you will find them at the Poor Relation."

Mr. Davenport goggled.

"Now if the young miss, the *soi-disant* Hungarian of royal blood, were in peril, I am sure Lord Eston would ride to the rescue and the circumstances would jolt his affections into something warmer."

"Peril? What peril? Eston's a good shot. Don't want my head blown off."

"As I said, I think you will find your Hungarians are part and parcel of the odd lot who run the Poor Relation. If that is the case, you tell the villainous Bonnard of Tupple's that it was the younger one who did the damage to his hotel with the dead cat. When he has finished raging, you sympathize with him and say if it were you, you would kidnap young Miss Hungarian and tell the owners of the Poor Relation—in an anonymous note, of course—that unless they put a notice in the *Morning Post* to the effect that the Poor Relation is closing down for good, then she will be killed."

"I say, you do have some Gothic ideas. Not quite my style. Why do you not do this yourself?"

"I would not be believed. Do you really want Miss Boyle?"

"Yes, she's the prettiest thing I ever set eyes on."

"Then you have to do only a very little—a word here, a word there."

"Ho, and what if Bonnard kills this Hungarian?"

"I shall employ men to watch him. She will have a bad fright but come to no harm."

"I say, what if she really is a member of the Hungarian royalty?"

"I shall eat my hat."

Mr. Davenport left and Mr. Glennon crossed to the

window to watch him go. Pity the boy wasn't like his father, thought Mr. Glennon, shaking his head. But what Aubrey Davenport needed was not an heiress, he had money enough, nor a woman of good sense, for he had little himself, but a dainty feather-brain like Amanda Boyle. They were perfectly matched. All the clever schemes, such as getting rid of Mrs. Boyle's sister, which Aubrey thought his own, had been planted in his brain by Mr. Glennon, whose one joy in life was manipulating other people while congratulating himself on his own cunning.

"Mr. Davenport!" cried Amanda later that day. "What a surprise. You have become quite a stranger."

He was pleased to find her alone. "Where are your parents?"

She pouted. "Mama is as cross as anything because her sister, my Aunt Tabitha, is not dying at all and has already left for Bath. So she and Papa have gone to see someone, I don't know who, and I am glad they are gone because Papa was accusing Mama of being silly, having left the visit to Aunt too late, and she was accusing him of being a tyrant. Still, I shall soon be married and have a home of my own."

"And children?"

She blushed. "Really, Mr. Davenport, it is very unlike you to bring up subjects unsuited for a lady's ears!"

"I am sorry. I think you are very brave and courageous."

Her eyes widened. "Why?"

"Eston is a very powerful, very lusty man. You are so fragile and delicate."

"Lord Eston is a complete gentleman and does not thrust his attentions on me."

"Of course not. That he will do after his marriage. His patience is astounding. When his late mistress, Mrs. Bagshot, told me she could not . . . er . . . keep up with his passions, I feared for you."

"What are you talking about?" Amanda's voice was shrill with fear.

"Forgive me. To me, you are a goddess. You are like a piece of fine Dresden china. I would not see you harmed."

"Harmed?" Amanda's voice had risen to a squeak.

"I go too far. Some men have dark passions and darker practices. Ah, me."

The now thoroughly terrified Amanda looked at him with dilated eyes. Young ladies were not supposed to know of coarse things. But with so many prostitutes in the streets and so many men in their cups consorting openly and amorously with these women, it was hard not to know a few facts of life. And yet she had thought that gentlemen confined their lusts to the lower orders of women. And yet his mistress could not cope with his passions!

There had been an anger and impatience about Lord Eston these days when he spoke to her. Sometimes, it seemed to Amanda, he looked at her with dislike. But now she thought she knew the reason for those brooding, smouldering looks.

She confided her fears to her mother later that day. Mrs. Boyle was in a bad temper. She could not believe her own sister had escaped her. She listened with half an ear to her daughter's trembling confidences and then said impatiently, "You are marrying a *man*, not that pug of yours. Of course you will have to submit to love-making. All women do. No woman, or rather no lady, enjoys it. You just grit your teeth and think of something else."

The following day, Mr. Davenport saw Cassandra leaving the Poor Relation, and although she immediately swung round and presented her back to him, he had seen enough to know it was she. He drove straight to Tupple's and was soon telling an amazed and furious Bonnard the name of the person behind the near downfall of his hotel.

Bonnard's rage knew no bounds. In order to entice customers back to the hotel, he had had to outlay a great deal of money. He listened carefully to Mr. Davenport's suggestion of kidnap and then quietened slightly. "Can't go about kidnapping royalty," he said.

"She ain't royalty, I'm sure," replied Mr. Davenport. "More likely a servant at the Poor Relation that these old frights who run it sent round here to gull you."

Bonnard pulled himself together and said quietly he was grateful for the information. Then, when Mr. Davenport had left, he sent out his spies. The servants at the Poor Relation had been warned against spies from Tupple's but naturally thought they were not to talk about menus or prices. So a pretty chambermaid, accosted by a handsome waiter from Tupple's, chatted freely about this Miss Blessop, niece of Miss Tonks, one of the partners.

Bonnard checked on the Blessops. Rich gentry, not aristocracy. He soon also had the intelligence that Miss Cassandra Blessop had run away from home and was in disgrace with her parents.

Lord Eston was dressing to go out two days later when his butler informed him that there was a person desiring to see him. "I don't see persons," said Lord Eston tetchily. He was to take Amanda driving and he wondered if he could bear another afternoon of her prattle without strangling her.

The butler hesitated and then said, "Although the lady comes without a maid, she has the appearance of a genteel spinster."

"Probably collecting for some charity," said Lord

Eston. "Put her in the downstairs saloon and give her tea and tell her I will grant her two minutes."

He was amazed when he finally entered the saloon to see Miss Tonks, sitting on the very edge of a chair, clutching a large reticule and with her eyes red with weeping.

"Cassandra!" he said, fear clutching at his heart.

Miss Tonks covered her face and began to weep.

He knelt down in front of her and took her hands away from her face. "You must pull yourself together. It is Cassandra, is it not? Something has happened to Cassandra?"

She nodded dumbly and then began to cry harder than ever. Swearing under his breath, he rang the bell and ordered brandy and then held a glass to Miss Tonks's pale lips and ordered her harshly to drink it. She gulped some down and then choked, but her sobs gradually grew quieter.

"She . . . she has been kidnapped. We got a letter saying that if we did not announce the Poor Relation was going out of business, then we would never see her again. I told the others I would ask you for help and Sir Philip said he would deal with it and not to tell anyone, but I am so *afraid*."

"Her parents? Surely her parents have snatched her?"

"Honoria would not order us to close down. Sir Philip said it was Tupple's."

"Tupple's. Bonnard. Leave it to me, Miss Tonks. If that cur knows where she is, I will shake it out of him."

"But you must not tell Sir Philip. He said he had it all in hand. But he is so flamboyant and so determined to get revenge on Tupple's that he might put Cassandra's life at risk."

"Miss Tonks, go back and say nothing."

When the weeping spinster had been ushered out, Lord Eston took a pistol out of the drawer of his desk and primed it. He felt numb and cold. He had kept away from

Cassandra out of duty. Damn duty! If he ever saw her again, he would not let her go.

He drove to Tupple's, walked into the entrance hall and demanded to see Mr. Bonnard. After a wait of some ten minutes, a servant came back to say Mr. Bonnard was not in the hotel.

Forcing a smile on his face, Lord Eston said calmly, "What a pity. I was going to invest money in this hotel. But if he is not interested enough to see me . . ."

"It could be, my lord," said the servant quickly, "that Mr. Bonnard has come back in by the rear entrance. Pray be so kind as to wait a little longer."

Lord Eston waited grimly.

In a few minutes, Bonnard himself appeared. "My lord!" he cried. "I am just this moment returned. A glass of wine? We have some fine claret. You will not find better—"

"Is there somewhere we can be private?" said Lord Eston. "I wish to talk business."

Bonnard's eyes gleamed. "Come this way, my lord. I have a private parlour upstairs."

As the hotelier led Lord Eston upstairs, he experienced a sudden qualm and was conscious of the girl he had locked securely in one of the attics. This Eston had been a friend of the supposed Hungarian ladies, which followed that Eston must have known what they were up to. He turned and looked back. Lord Eston smiled at him blandly. Bonnard gave a mental shrug. What could this well-barbered, well-tailored lily of the field do to such as himself?

He led the way into his parlour but left the door open.

"Now, my lord," he began.

Lord Eston drew the pistol from his pocket and levelled it at the startled hotelier.

"Now, Bonnard," he said, "you will take me quietly to

where you have Miss Cassandra Blessop hidden or I will blow your brains out."

"Who?"

Lord Eston moved like lightning and punched him savagely on the side of his face. "I have no time for your lies."

"What are you doing? I have only to call for help."

"You'd be dead before anyone reached this room. Kidnapping is a hanging offence. Move!"

Bonnard looked at him grimly. If he led this lord to where Cassandra was, then he, Bonnard, would stand trial and be hanged. So why should he fear a bullet through the brain?

Lord Eston put the pistol in his pocket. "I see you no longer fear death by shooting. But I shall beat the intelligence I require out of you."

Bonnard darted for the door. Lord Eston tripped him up and he went flying.

"Now," said Lord Eston, kneeling on his chest and seizing an oil-lamp from the desk. "Let's just empty this over you and set you alight and see if you might scream the truth in your death agonies." He poured the oil over Mr. Bonnard's face and then, holding him down with one hand, took out his tinder-box and struck it.

"No," screamed Bonnard. "The attic!"

Lord Eston jumped to his feet. He seized the key from the lock and locked Mr. Bonnard in and then ran for the stairs.

"Cassandra!" he shouted when he reached the top of the house. He tried door after door until he found a locked one and, standing back, kicked at the lock with his boot until the door splintered and sagged open, hanging crazily on its hinges.

Cassandra was tied to a chair in the middle of the room, with a cruel gag about her mouth.

He untied the gag and kissed her, kissed her with all the pent-up longing and passion of wasted months. "Please untie me," said Cassandra when she could. "Oh, I am so glad to see you. I have been so very frightened. I feel dirty and I am so hungry."

He released her bonds and raised her to her feet and caught her in his arms. He wound the long strands of her red hair in his fingers and smiled down at her freckled face. "You are beautiful," he said. "Marry me."

"Why?"

"Because I love you."

"Then why are you engaged to Miss Boyle?"

"I'm a fool. Kiss me, Cassandra."

She looked searchingly into his eyes and then, with a little sigh, she wound her arms about him and kissed him full on the mouth. He felt the attic room whirling about him and clung tightly to her as if for support. Then he said raggedly, "We must go. I locked Bonnard in his parlour. If he gets out, he may come after us. How did he get you?"

"I went out to the shops and a closed carriage came alongside. The door opened and then a man grabbed me and dragged me in. Bonnard was in the carriage and held a knife to my throat."

"I'll see him hang at Newgate." He lifted her in his arms and carried her out. "Very romantic," giggled Cassandra, "but not enough room on this narrow stair for you to carry me. I can walk."

They went down together, his arm about her shoulders. Cassandra felt the nightmare was over.

And then, when they reached the head of the main staircase leading down to the hall, they found themselves face-to-face with Bonnard. Behind him were the most evil-looking of his servants. He was carrying a great horse pistol.

"Take them," he ordered, as Lord Eston thrust Cassandra behind him.

And then suddenly there was a huge angry howl and a shattering of glass. "The mob," screamed a servant who was farther down the staircase. "They've shattered the doors."

"Kill the Bonapartist bastard," called a voice and the cry was taken up from below and then reverberated along the street outside.

Bonnard's servants scattered. The hotelier turned an ugly colour with fright. He suddenly dropped his pistol and thrust his way past Lord Eston and Cassandra and leaped for the upper staircase.

"I do not know which is the more terrifying, Bonnard or the mob," said Lord Eston. "Keep close to me and walk very slowly and bravely towards them."

The hall was swarming with drunken men who were smashing everything in sight. Slowly Cassandra and Lord Eston walked down.

And then a voice shouted, "Make way for Lord Eston, the hero of the Peninsula!"

A great roar of "Aye. A hero," went up.

The mob parted as they walked through the hall, doffing their caps and grinning.

It was like walking through wild beasts, thought Lord Eston. The mob outside cheered them as well, surging forward as they passed, all trying to get into the hotel.

And then suddenly they were clear. "The militia will be along in a minute," said Lord Eston. "Nearly home. There's my brave girl. Thank God some fool took me for a hero."

"Not some fool," said Cassandra between laughter and tears. "That dirty old man who was leading the mob was Sir Philip Sommerville."

★ ★ ★

"Nonsense," said Lady Fortescue, pouring tea with a steady hand. "Sir Philip did very well. Now you must admit, Lord Eston, that you would have been hard put to it to take Cassandra out of there without Sir Philip's help."

"But the guests," exclaimed Lord Eston. "What of the hotel guests?"

"Well, you know," said Lady Fortescue, "there were only two parties and Sir Philip warned them earlier that Bonnard was a Bonapartist spy and to leave quietly and take their belongings without telling anyone why they were leaving."

"And is Bonnard a Bonapartist spy?"

"I neither know nor care," said Lady Fortescue. "I doubt the man is even French. Such a good idea of Sir Philip's. So easy to rouse the mob these days. They are always rioting about something. Do try the seed-cake, Lord Eston."

"Where is Cassandra now?" asked Mrs. Budley.

"She is with her aunt. She is washing and changing. She will be with us presently. As, I trust, will Sir Philip, although I think the idea of leading a riot appeals to him. I do hope he does not go too far."

"Lady Fortescue," said Lord Eston severely, "I think they can go no further. No doubt by now they have wrecked the hotel and hanged Bonnard from his own chandelier."

"Which will save the state paying for it," said Colonel Sandhurst.

The door opened and Cassandra and Miss Tonks came in. Lord Eston stood up and opened his arms and Cassandra ran into them.

Lady Fortescue's voice was acid. "Remember where you are, Lord Eston, and release Miss Blessop immediately."

Lord Eston swung round and, holding Cassandra by the hand, said, "We are to be married."

"Indeed! You are sure?" Lady Fortescue surveyed the couple and then smiled. "Yes, I can see you are sure. Goodness, here is Sir Philip in time to hear the good news. Sir Philip, Lord Eston and Miss Blessop are to be married."

Sir Philip, a small bundle of foul-smelling rags, sank wearily into a chair. "Oh," he said indifferently. "Well, to more exciting news. My mob took Tupple's apart. Bonnard's fled. No one was hurt. I told 'em to leave the servants alone. I got everyone dispersed before the militia rode up."

"Had we not better now inform the authorities of the kidnapping of Miss Blessop?" asked Lord Eston.

Sir Philip flicked him a contemptuous look. "Start too many scandals and inquiries. I'm not a hanging man myself, even for such a cur as Bonnard. Too much hanging. Too . . ." His eyes closed and he fell asleep and began to snore.

Chapter Eight

I'll frighten her into marriage.
—JOHN BENN JOHNSTONE

IN THE cold light of day, Lord Eston realized that somehow he must see Amanda alone and get her to break the engagement. If she would not, then he would have to break it himself and he felt sure that Boyle would immediately and gleefully sue him for breach of promise. He waited in Mr. Davenport's large but singularly unornamented house while the butler went to see whether Miss Boyle would receive him. Lighter spaces on the walls showed where pictures had hung. There were hardly any ornaments. Obviously Mr. Davenport was taking no chances with the light-fingered Mr. Boyle in residence. The butler was gone a long time and there were sounds of an altercation coming from abovestairs.

At last the butler returned and said the ladies would be pleased to receive him. When he entered the drawing-room, Amanda was playing with her pug, Rupert, her cheeks pink, and Mrs. Boyle was looking militant.

"I wonder if I might have a few words with my fiancée . . . alone," said Lord Eston. "Just a few," said Mrs.

Boyle, rising to her feet and ignoring her daughter's squeak of protest. She went out and left the door open.

"My Rupert is very brave," said Amanda, holding up the wheezing pug. "And . . . and very jealous. He does not like it when gentlemen come near me."

"Then I shall stay here on the other side of the room and say what I have to say." Lord Eston looked at her curiously. She was as adorable as ever in appearance but he wondered what he had ever seen in her.

"My dear," he began, and then stopped. For the first time, he noticed that Amanda was really afraid of him and not just playing some silly flirtatious game.

Hope began to rise. "Amanda," he said, "do pay attention to me. I feel somehow that you are not looking forward to our marriage. This is the first time we have been alone in a long time. Would you not like to release me from the engagement?"

Amanda kept her head down and stroked the little dog's coat. "Mama and Papa want me to have a title," she said finally.

"But you do not want me and I do not want an unwilling bride. I think I know how to go about it. Let me have a talk with your mother and I feel I can arrange things."

"Oh, could you?" she breathed. "I would be most grateful. We are not at all suited, you know."

"As a matter of interest, what is it about me that disgusts you?"

Amanda coloured prettily. "You do not disgust me. There is just something . . ."

"Never mind. When your mother returns, leave us together."

Just at that moment, Mrs. Boyle entered the room. Amanda murmured something, scooped up her dog and left them.

"I fear I have distressed your daughter," said Lord

Eston, "but she must be made to see sense. Just because there is no longer going to be a large wedding . . ."

"Why on earth not?" demanded Mrs. Boyle sharply.

Mr. Boyle came into the room and joined them.

"Hear this, Mr. Boyle," said his wife. "Eston has just been telling me that our Amanda isn't to have a big wedding."

"Why not?"

"The fact is I have been speculating wildly," said Lord Eston, "and left a great hole in my fortune. I will have to sell my town house and live quietly in the country. But with hard work and great economies, I know I can come about." Mr. Davenport, who had been about to join them, listened eagerly just outside the door.

"This is not what we planned for our daughter," exclaimed Mr. Boyle.

"It is not what any of us had planned, Mr. Boyle, but I cannot conjure up a fortune just like that. It will take years of hard drudgery on my estates to repair the damage. Amanda will have to live quietly in the country." Mr. Davenport turned slightly. Amanda had crept up beside him and was listening as well.

"She will of course not be bored. She can perform many good works," said Lord Eston, gleefully hammering the last nail in the coffin of his engagement.

Mr. Davenport took Amanda firmly by the hand and led her into the room. "Lord Eston," he said, "this is not the time for you to be thinking of marrying such a frail and beautiful lady and exposing her to the indignity of debt and duns."

"I suppose you want to marry her yourself," said Lord Eston.

The Boyles, all of them, looked at Mr. Davenport with hope.

"If Miss Boyle will release you from your engagement,

then I will marry her," he said. "The wedding is arranged. But let it go ahead. I will be the bridegroom."

"Oh, that would be much more sensible," lisped Amanda.

"It's a good thing I didn't pay over your dowry," said Mr. Boyle. "I'm disappointed in you, Eston."

"It seems to me that Miss Boyle wishes to be released," said Lord Eston. "I will send a notice to the newspapers to that effect."

"What a narrow escape!" cried Mr. Boyle, when Lord Eston, acting suitably downcast, had taken his leave. He rubbed his hands with glee. What pickings he would have out of Davenport's vast fortune.

Honoria Blessop was a most unhappy woman. Her conscience, which had previously never troubled her overmuch, was rampant. She was haunted by pictures of her daughter lying dead in some ditch. Pride had stopped her from telling the authorities to start a search. She had been so sure Cassandra would come to her senses.

Guilt weighed heavily on her. She had been a bad woman. She had told Edward that Letitia had no dowry so that Edward would transfer his affections to her, which he had done. She had told her dying parents that a simple will was enough. She as the elder would handle everything, make Letitia a generous allowance and give her a Season in London. And she had not.

After five miscarriages, she had at last produced a son, named Edward after his father, and, a year later, a daughter, Cassandra, and had dreamt of social triumphs when her daughter grew to beauty. She had set her heart on this ambition so much that she had only put up a token protest when, at the age of sixteen, young Edward had left to join the navy. As a young child, Cassandra had been blessed with glossy brown hair. But by her sixth year, it had turned red and continued to grow redder and redder. She had never quite been able to forgive Cassandra for having such red hair. Now she had driven her only daughter to ruin. A lifetime of despising Letitia could not be changed. How could such a feckless weakling as Letitia protect a young girl?

Her husband came in and found her at her usual position by the window, waiting for the post-boy, waiting for news.

He was sober for the first time in a long time and he looked at her seriously. "Mrs. Blessop," he said quietly, "enough is enough. A search for Cassandra must begin immediately."

Honoria nodded dumbly and took out a small handkerchief and wiped her eyes.

The post-boy's horn sounded at the end of the drive and one of the little maids went scampering down to meet him.

Honoria went very still as she watched the girl returning holding a letter. If only God would give her back her lost daughter, then she would make amends to Edward and Letitia for all her cruelty.

She rose as the maid entered the room, and snatched the letter and broke the seal.

She scanned the contents and then slowly sank into a chair and read the letter slowly and carefully, her face darkening with anger.

"What is it?" asked Edward.

She held out the letter. "It's from Letitia," she said in a colourless voice.

He read it through and then he began to laugh. "Good old Letitia," he cried. "She's done what you could never do. She's gone and got Cassandra engaged to Lord Eston. Why, woman, what ails you? Our girl is safe and well and happy. Eston is coming here to ask my permission, and Letitia is bringing Cassandra home!"

I will never forgive Letitia, thought Honoria. She did this to spite me!

Some days later Amanda and Mr. Davenport were driving through the Park, each dressed in the height of fashion. "So you forgive me for having taken you away from Eston?" he asked.

"Oh, yes," said Amanda with a little shudder. "You *saved* me. He was so disappointed, of course, so furious, that he went off and got engaged to that Hungarian who is not a Hungarian at all, but a hurly-burly girl who likes to play tricks."

"They will be well suited, my little love."

"I rather liked Miss Blessop. Perhaps I should warn her about Eston as you warned me."

"Oh, no," said Mr. Davenport with a sudden picture of pistols at dawn. "Do not do that. Think of our wedding instead!"

The wedding of Lord Eston to Miss Cassandra Blessop was a quiet affair, punctuated by the sobbing of her mother. Honoria felt that Lord Eston should have known better than to have invited those freaks from the hotel. Cassandra had sealed her mother's misery by making her aunt a maid of honour.

Cassandra was aware of only her husband at the wedding breakfast. She was married and she would live happily ever after.

Amanda, her parents, and Mr. Davenport were also guests, the quietness of the wedding seeming to bear out Lord Eston's story about penury. Amanda was still to be married, and although she sometimes wished she were to have a title, for such as Cassandra would take precedence over her at social functions, she was happy with her adoring Aubrey Davenport. But she felt sorry for Cassandra, who seemed a good-hearted, jolly sort of lady. The fact that Cassandra was cursed with unfashionable red hair made Amanda feel even warmer towards her. Poor innocent, thought Amanda, I really ought to warn her. Whatever Aubrey may say, I should have warned her before about Eston.

And so, during the dancing after the wedding breakfast, when Cassandra went upstairs to change out of her wedding dress, Amanda followed her.

Six months later, Lord and Lady Eston sat down to a late breakfast in their country home. Cassandra stared at her husband for a few moments and then said in a thin voice, "I wish you would not eat boiled eggs."

"Why not?"

"Because you tap, tap, tap at the shell with your spoon and it irritates me. Now I come to think of it, there are many things about you that irritate me."

"The feeling is mutual," he said, glaring at her. "Do you have to crumble your toast in that fidgety way?"

What Cassandra was really saying was, "Why did you dance twice with pretty little Freda Hamilton at the ball last night?" And what he was in fact replying was, "You were a bit too much taken with the charms of that tall guardsman for my liking." But neither of them had yet learned the hard lesson that married couples usually fight over anything but the thing that is really bothering them.

"I'll eat my toast any way I like," said Cassandra, thinking, he doesn't love me anymore.

"Then leave me to have my breakfast in peace. Eat the way you like, and mind your own damned business."

Lord Eston ducked under the table as the coffee-pot went sailing over his head.

Then he rose, walked to the end of the table and jerked his red-haired wife to her feet and shook her and she retaliated by kicking him hard on the shins.

Then she slapped him hard.

Both stood staring at each other in shocked silence.

"I . . . I am sorry," whispered Cassandra.

"Prove it."

She kissed the end of his nose.

"More."

She kissed his mouth.

He swung her up into his arms and headed for the door.

"Where are we going?" laughed Cassandra.

"Where do you think?"

Half an hour later, Cassandra wriggled her naked body into a more comfortable position under his and said with a giggle, "I never told you, but your precious Amanda warned me against you."

"What? What did she say?"

"She hinted you had dark and passionate lusts."

"And what did you say?"

"Good!"

"Minx, kiss me again!"

Sir Philip had sold the necklace, but not the diamond tiara. Now funds were desperately needed again. He could hardly believe they had all got through so much money. He went to his favourite jeweller and completed the deal to their mutual satisfaction. No need for Miss Tonks to dither on about paying her sister back. Lord Eston had bought his mother-in-law a new diamond tiara and necklace.

In the shadows outside the shop, Bonnard watched him. He had been watching the Poor Relation Hotel for months, plotting revenge, hoping for revenge. He felt sure it was they who had incited the mob against him. Now he was nearly destitute, and hunger fueled his rage. He now knew Sir Philip by sight. This was the first time Sir Philip had ventured away from the genteel streets of the West End and into an area where it might be easy to attack him.

Peering in the shop, Bonnard had seen the diamonds and seen the tiara. Greed was added to his anger. He waited until Sir Philip emerged and followed him until a crazy old building hanging over the street blotted out the sun.

He ran forward and brought his cudgel down hard on Sir Philip's head.

"Hey!" shouted a voice and he could hear the rattle of the watch sounding from the end of the street. He stooped over Sir Philip's crumpled body and seized the money from his pocket. He threw down the cudgel and ran for his life, fleeing through the twisting, smelly streets where starved, white faces stared at him curiously from rat-infested buildings.

Miss Tonks was never to forget that awful day when an unconscious Sir Philip was borne into the Poor Relation on a door. The watch had found his address in a notebook in his pocket. Sir Philip looked as small as a child. Colonel Sandhurst had him carried to a vacant guest bedroom and sent for the physician while Mrs. Budley, Miss Tonks, and Lady Fortescue sat beside the bed, bathing Sir Philip's forehead and praying for his life.

For days the old man seemed to hang between life and death. Miss Tonks could not be moved from the bedside. She had a truckle-bed set up in Sir Philip's room, where she snatched a little sleep between looking after her patient.

And then, quite suddenly, he rallied. At first, he was weak and feeble and spoke little above a whisper. Then he began to suggest that champagne was what was needed to restore him. Then he began to tease Miss Tonks unmercifully about "having slept with him." And finally he became his irascible, nasty old self.

That was when they discovered that what they had feared was true: that he had been robbed of the money they so desperately needed.

"Did you see who struck you down?" asked Lady Fortescue.

"I've told you and told you," snapped Sir Philip, "I don't know. Now what are we to do?"

"I did my best," said Miss Tonks. "It's not my fault you lost the stupid money."

"Nor mine neither, you withered old hag," said Sir Philip.

"Really, sir," complained the colonel. "I swear you owe your life to Miss Tonks. Never had a man a more devoted nurse."

"Sorry," mumbled Sir Philip. "But, demme, I ask if it is worth going on with all this. I mean, we always seem to be embroiled in frights and troubles. What about Eston? He's worth a bob or too."

"Lord Eston knew he was paying us in a way when he bought Honoria that set of diamonds," said Miss Tonks.

"Well, I'm tired," said Sir Philip. "I can't do any more."

"We are all tired," said Miss Tonks. "We could sell the hotel—it is a thriving business—and have plenty to lead a quiet life, perhaps in the country."

"With pigs round the door?" Sir Philip sneered. "I am not yet ready to rot in some country slum."

"If we had one more year," said Lady Fortescue, "and budget this time, budget carefully. We have been spending money like water. We had enough out of that necklace to set all of us up for life. But I do not want to give in. Someone had better go and steal something."

"Not I," said Miss Tonks. "Not again."

"Tell you what," said the colonel, "we'll draw straws."

Reluctantly the others agreed.

Let it not be me, prayed Miss Tonks. I did not tell the others, but Cassandra offered me a home and I refused. If only I had taken her offer!

I don't mind drawing the short straw, thought Sir Philip. I'll just fake a relapse and wait until they send someone else.

Not me, thought the colonel nervously. It's all right for Sir Philip. I'm not cut out for a life of crime. I'm beginning to hate this hotel. I want to be a gentleman again. But only if Lady Fortescue comes with me.

I'm old and tired, mused Lady Fortescue, but if it's me, then I'll need to go ahead with it. I should be planning my funeral. Not living from hand to mouth. But the hotel was her pride and joy and she did not really want to leave it.

Mrs. Budley sat silent, wide eyes watching as Sir Philip went to get the straws. She had a comfortable feeling she would be safe. It was the others who were always involved in dangers and alarms.

Sir Philip brought the straws in. One by one they picked one out. Miss Tonks looked down at the long straw in her hands and thanked God for deliverance. The colonel smiled at his long straw and laid it carefully on the table beside Lady Fortescue's equally long straw. Let that rascal, Sir Philip, cope. But Sir Philip had a long straw as well.

So that left . . .

Mrs. Budley sat with her head bowed, twisting the short straw this way and that in her trembling fingers.

One by one the others rose and left the room. It was, thought Mrs. Budley, like being a shamed army officer being left alone by his comrades in a room with a loaded revolver.

She sat for a long time by herself and then she rose and

went downstairs. She would not talk about it, would not refer to it, and then perhaps the others would forget.

Mr. Boyle thought he would surely go to heaven when he died, for he was spending his time in hell now. Somehow Mr. Davenport's man of business had persuaded him that he and Mrs. Boyle should not subject the rest of their children to the rigours of a sea voyage and then had gone about finding schools for Amanda's two brothers and three sisters.

The shock of finding there actually was a Heatherington plantation had not left him. The fact that the overseer, Jamie Macdonald, a ferociously jolly Scotchman, seemed determined to oversee *him* added to his misery. Jamie was always there at six in the morning with his great braying laugh, suggesting they get to work before the heat of the day became too intense. What was worse was that Mr. Davenport's man of business had had the folly to free the slaves and make them paid servants, and so he could not take his temper out on them any more than he could on an English servant, in fact less, because that document he had so gleefully signed, promising everything, had a clause in the small print saying that all servants were to be treated with courtesy.

He wrote long and bitter letters to Mr. Davenport, but Mr. Glennon was the one who always replied, reminding him of his contract.

Mrs. Boyle surprisingly adapted quite quickly to the heat and to the local society. It was all right for *her,* he thought bitterly. All she had to do with her time was to drive out in the carriage, making calls.

And then, after the first year, a year during which he had dreamt of nothing but taking revenge on his son-in-law, the plantation began to pay, began to flourish. He discounted the fact that it had anything to do with the hard-working Jamie and slowly began to grow proud of it. Soon he was awake and ready when Jamie arrived for him. He was praised by the other plantation owners on his success. Anti-slavery campaigners made a pilgrimage to see him, hailing him as enlightened, and he would brag about how he had freed the slaves himself.

Mr. Davenport had been bracing himself for his father-in-law's return at the end of three years and was amazed when Mr. Boyle finally wrote to him saying that he liked the life and climate of Jamaica and preferred to stay.